Lizzie McGuire
OFFICIAL EPISODE GUIDE

By Heidi Hurst
Based on the series
created by Terri Minksy

Watch it on

New York

A special shout-out to
Stan Rogow, *Lizzie McGuire* Executive Producer
Cathryn Wagner, *Lizzie McGuire* Costume Designer
for providing production trivia

Copyright © 2004 Disney Enterprises, Inc.
address Disney Press, 114 Fifth Avenue, New York, New York 10011-5690.

Printed in the United States of America

First Edition
1 3 5 7 9 10 8 6 4 2

Library of Congress Control Number: 2004107696

ISBN 0-7868-4663-1

For more Disney Press fun, visit www.disneybooks.com
Visit DisneyChannel.com

WELCOME TO THE WONDERFUL WORLD OF ...
LIZZIE!

Lizzie McGuire is a television show about the life of
a girl and her two loyal best friends, who help her
endure such ongoing dramas as heartbreaking
crushes, she-beast cheerleaders, totally humiliating
moments, and completely embarrassing parents.
Viewers always know what Lizzie's thinking—
because her animated alter ego tells us!

> You can totally say
> that again!

Sixty-five episodes of the show were produced,
and this is your guide to every one of them.
Each entry includes a summary of the episode,
and a "Did You Know?" section, which
lists interesting trivia about it. Just for fun,
there's also a "Can You Spot the Bloopers?" section,
which challenges you to look for the goofs yourself!

So, turn the page and start reading about the
longtime #1 most popular kids' cable television show
and two-time winner of the Nickelodeon Kids'
Choice Awards for Favorite TV Show—
Lizzie McGuire!

CONTENTS

DIRECTOR: Larry Shaw
WRITER: Terri Minsky
EXECUTIVE PRODUCERS: Terri Minsky & Stan Rogow
PRODUCER: John Whitman
SERIES CREATED BY: Terri Minsky
CAST STARS: Hilary Duff (Lizzie McGuire),
Lalaine (Miranda Sanchez),
Adam Lamberg
(David "Gordo" Gordon),
Jake Thomas (Matt McGuire),
Hallie Todd (Jo McGuire), and
Robert Carradine (Sam McGuire)
COSTARS: Dot-Marie Jones (Coach Kelly),
Bryon Fox (Danny Kessler),
Ashlie Brillault (Kate Sanders),
Jennifer Nicole Freeman (Alix)

EPISODE NUMBER 1: "POOL PARTY"

WHAT HAPPENS?

On the school bus, Lizzie McGuire and her best friend Miranda Sanchez are invited to a pool party by their crush, Danny Kessler. They are excited to go. But Lizzie's mother tells her she can't because the pool party is the same day as Nana's 80th birthday.

The next day at school, popular snob Kate Sanders buddies up to Miranda because she heard Miranda's mother can draw temporary Mehndi tattoos, and Kate wants one. When Miranda ignores Lizzie to talk to Kate, Lizzie is insulted. Then Miranda admits that she'll still go to the pool party even though Lizzie can't, and Lizzie feels betrayed.

Lizzie's mom eventually gives her permission to go to the pool party because Nana decides to spend her birthday in Las Vegas. But Lizzie doesn't go. Instead, she hangs out with her friend Gordo at home, tie-dyeing her sheets. Gordo convinces Lizzie to forgive Miranda, and he surprises Lizzie by telling her he thinks of her as his best friend. Later, Miranda stops by after the party, having had a terrible time without Lizzie. They vow to be best friends again.

6

DID YOU KNOW?

Jump in, the water's fine! (Yeah, right.)

- Even though this "pilot" episode was the first one filmed, it was actually broadcast third—after the "Picture Day" and "Rumors" episodes.

- The original, working title for the *Lizzie McGuire* TV series was *What's Lizzie Thinking?*

- This episode was voted a Top 5 favorite Lizzie episode in a 2004 Disney Online poll. Position number: 2.

- In this episode, viewers learn Lizzie has known Gordo since she was one day old.

- Viewers also learn that Kate, Lizzie, and Miranda used to be friends, but when Kate went through puberty, she became popular and outgrew her old friends.

- Jennifer Nicole Freeman, Neutrogena spokesmodel and star of *My Wife and Kids,* plays Kate's friend.

CAN YOU SPOT THE BLOOPERS?

- After Danny invites Lizzie and Miranda to the pool party and they're celebrating, Lalaine (who plays Miranda) looks directly at the camera, which normally wouldn't make it into the final cut.

- When Lizzie is standing at her locker, she looks at her bracelet, hanging from a hook. She turns around, and when she turns back, the bracelet is no longer in her locker!

EPISODE NUMBER 2: "PICTURE DAY"

DIRECTOR: Neal Israel
WRITERS: Douglas Tuber & Tim Maile
EXECUTIVE PRODUCERS: Stan Rogow & Susan Estelle Jansen
CONSULTING PRODUCERS: Douglas Tuber & Tim Maile
PRODUCER: Jill Danton
SERIES CREATED BY: Terri Minsky
CAST STARS: Hilary Duff (Lizzie McGuire),
Lalaine (Miranda Sanchez),
Adam Lamberg
(David "Gordo" Gordon),
Jake Thomas (Matt McGuire),
Hallie Todd (Jo McGuire), and
Robert Carradine (Sam McGuire)
GUEST STAR: Sonya Eddy (Photographer)
COSTARS: Ashlie Brillault (Kate Sanders),
Clayton Snyder (Ethan),
Chelsea J. Wilson (Parker McKenzie),
Aaron Fors (Ed)

WHAT HAPPENS?

Today is one of the biggest days at school—picture day! Lizzie is trying to decide on the perfect outfit when her mother insists she wear a lame unicorn sweater, a gift from Gammy McGuire. Lizzie wears the sweater, but she spends half the school day trying to find something else to wear for the camera. And Lizzie's not the only one with problems. Miranda and Kate show up at school wearing the exact same outfit (talk about bad karma!). Meanwhile, Gordo is under pressure from Mr. Cool, Ethan Craft, to look "tough" in his school picture.

Back at the McGuire house, Matt fakes an illness to get out of a pop quiz, but Mrs. McGuire catches on and forces him to eat borscht and wind a ball of yarn.

At school, Gordo borrows a totally cool white blouse from the drama club for Lizzie to wear. Then in art class, Kate persuades Ed the school nerd to "spill" paint on Miranda's outfit. Lizzie jumps in front of Miranda, saving her best friend from the "paint grenade." Lizzie, however, is now splattered with green paint! Nonetheless, she happily poses for the camera—the perfect picture of friendship.

DID YOU KNOW?

How can I appear cool when I'm wearing a sweater that makes me look like a cookie elf?

- In this episode, Gordo's hair is shorter and his voice is deeper than it is in the first episode.

- Viewers learn that Gammy McGuire is sixty-one and teaches windsurfing.

- When Lizzie is walking toward the bus, the song "Absolutely (Story of a Girl)" by Nine Days is played.

- Ethan Craft, future Lizzie and Miranda crush, is introduced in this episode, as is another recurring character, Parker McKenzie.

- Lizzie has a picture of Taylor Hanson, from the pop group Hanson, in her locker.

- In the original version of this episode, Matt raises his temperature on the thermometer by putting a penny in his mouth. But this was later changed to flashing a flashlight on the thermometer to raise his temp.

CAN YOU SPOT THE BLOOPERS?

- When Gordo is waiting to get his picture taken, Lizzie approaches him and calls him "Gordon" by mistake (in the script, the line reads "Gordo"). As the series progresses, it's clear that Ethan calls Gordo "Gordon," but Lizzie and Miranda never do.

- Lizzie describes her "Oops! . . . I Did It Again" outfit as a halter top, but when she's pictured in it, the shirt is a long-sleeved, red turtle-neck shirt.

- Mrs. McGuire tells Matt to go upstairs before she takes his temperature, but in the next scene he's in the living room downstairs, with a thermometer.

EPISODE NUMBER 3:
"RUMORS"

DIRECTOR: Neal Israel
WRITER: Melissa Gould
EXECUTIVE PRODUCERS: Stan Rogow & Susan Estelle Jansen
CONSULTING PRODUCERS: Douglas Tuber & Tim Maile
PRODUCER: Jill Danton
CAST STARS: Hilary Duff (Lizzie McGuire),
Lalaine (Miranda Sanchez),
Adam Lamberg
(David "Gordo" Gordon),
Jake Thomas (Matt McGuire),
Hallie Todd (Jo McGuire), and
Robert Carradine (Sam McGuire)
COSTARS: Ashlie Brillault (Kate Sanders),
Byron Fox (Danny Kessler),
Davida Williams (Claire Miller),
Taylor Gunnin (Head Cheerleader),
Mitchah Williams (Kid),
Britney Mitchell (Dancer),
Melissa Matthews (Dancer), and
Tiffany Burton (Dancer)

WHAT HAPPENS?

Lizzie tries out for cheerleading, but during tryouts it's obvious she isn't cut out for pom-poms. After hearing that Kate made the squad, Lizzie becomes jealous. That night, chatting online with Miranda, Lizzie types that the reason Kate made the squad was "because she stuffs her bra." Miranda accidentally forwards the message to all of their classmates.

The next day, Kate confronts Lizzie and Miranda to find out who spread the rumor. When Lizzie freezes in fear of Kate, Miranda takes the blame, so Kate declares war on Miranda. Lizzie feels bad, but Miranda and Gordo tell her she can't handle conflict like Miranda can. A series of mean tricks between Kate and Miranda embarrass both girls.

At home, Matt must take care of the class lizard. When his parents are supposed to watch over the lizard, it dies.

Meanwhile, Lizzie finally gathers her courage to confront Kate and tell her the truth. Kate and the cheerleaders retaliate by chanting a mean cheer at a pep rally, calling Lizzie a "loser." Lizzie is embarrassed, but she's proud that she finally stood up to Kate.

DID YOU KNOW?

🌸 "Rumors" was ranked as the third-highest-rated of all the *Lizzie* telecasts. (Ratings were measured among kids ages 6 to 11 on January 12, 2001.)

Gimme an L, gimme an I, gimme a . . . oh, just forget it!

🌸 Lizzie's online name is "Lizzee" and Miranda's name is "Mander."

🌸 Actress Lalaine, who plays Miranda, recalls her audition this way: "Disney was having a hard time finding someone for the part of Miranda Sanchez, so when I went in for the part, everyone else had already been in place. I went in for what I thought was a callback, as we were all doing a table reading and then I thought, wow, this is weird . . . I think I actually have the part right now!" And, of course, she did!

CAN YOU SPOT THE BLOOPERS?

🌸 At lunch, Gordo complains about the broccoli as he pushes it off his plate. But in a previous school lunch scene, students got to choose what food to put on their plates. If Gordo didn't like broccoli, why did he put in on his plate?

🌸 When Lizzie walks up to Kate in the gymnasium before the pep rally, a red "X" is on the floor. The "X" is to show actors where they should stand, but it is not supposed to be in the shot.

🌸 Lizzie types "Because Kate stuffs her bra" as her message, but when Miranda receives the message it says, "Kate stuffs her bra."

EPISODE NUMBER 4:
"I'VE GOT RHYTHMIC"

DIRECTOR: Alan Myerson
WRITER: Nancy Neufeld Callaway
EXECUTIVE PRODUCERS: Stan Rogow & Susan Estelle Jansen
CONSULTING PRODUCERS: Douglas Tuber & Tim Maile
PRODUCER: Jill Danton
SERIES CREATED BY: Terri Minsky
CAST STARS: Hilary Duff (Lizzie McGuire),
Lalaine (Miranda Sanchez),
Adam Lamberg
(David "Gordo" Gordon),
Jake Thomas (Matt McGuire),
Hallie Todd (Jo McGuire), and
Robert Carradine (Sam McGuire)
GUEST STARS: Dot-Marie Jones (Coach Kelly),
Ashlie Brillault (Kate Sanders),
Kyle J. Downes (Larry Tudgeman)
COSTARS: Brianna James (Super Smart Girl),
Michael Barryte (Super Smart Boy),
Larry Nicholas (Larry Stunt Double)

WHAT HAPPENS?

It's another day and another "B" for Lizzie. She wishes she were good at something, anything, and complains to Miranda and Gordo about being "average." But when gym class rolls around, she discovers her hidden talent: rhythmic gymnastics. Lizzie thinks it's a totally dorky sport, but when Coach Kelly tells her she should enter the regional competition, she decides to go for it.

She trains hard, wakes up at 5 A.M. every day, and is miserable. Her only motivation is that her rival Kate is jealous that Lizzie is better at something than she is. Kate won't stand for Lizzie being a star, so she sets out to destroy her performance at regionals. She enlists nerdy Larry Tudgeman to do the dirty work. Miranda and Gordo figure out what's up and save Lizzie from total embarrassment.

In the end, Lizzie's routine is excellent, but after the competition, she tells her parents she'd rather work hard at something she loves than be good at something she hates. Lizzie also realizes that she's not "average" as long as she's happy.

DID YOU KNOW?

> Why do I have to be so good at such a dorky sport?

- Toon Lizzie trivia: when the series was first being developed, voice-over was considered to express Lizzie's private thoughts. Using that idea as a springboard, the show's producers realized that an "animated" version of Lizzie's innermost thoughts could provide the show with a new approach to Lizzie's trials and tribulations. So "animated Lizzie" or "Toon Lizzie" was established as a regular part of each show.

- The show's writers were allowed to make Toon Lizzie morph, explode, melt, pull a canoe out of her backpack, or do almost anything—*almost*. Toon Lizzie could never be shown talking directly to the real Lizzie.

- This episode's title "I've Got Rhythmic" was inspired by the George Gershwin song, "I Got Rhythm."

- Larry Tudgeman makes his first appearance in this episode.

- Viewers learn that Lizzie bakes when she's upset about something.

CAN YOU SPOT THE BLOOPERS?

- At the gymnastics competition, Lizzie's school is announced as North Hills Junior High, but in later episodes, the name changes to Hillridge Junior High.

- When Lizzie is performing, the judges already have their scores for her in front of them!

13

EPISODE NUMBER 5:
"WHEN MOMS ATTACK"

DIRECTOR: Mark Rosman
WRITERS: Nina G. Bargiel & Jeremy J. Bargiel
EXECUTIVE PRODUCERS: Stan Rogow & Susan Estelle Jansen
CONSULTING PRODUCERS: Douglas Tuber & Tim Maile
PRODUCER: Jill Danton
SERIES CREATED BY: Terri Minsky
CAST STARS: Hilary Duff (Lizzie McGuire),
    Lalaine (Miranda Sanchez),
    Adam Lamberg
        (David "Gordo" Gordon),
    Jake Thomas (Matt McGuire),
    Hallie Todd (Jo McGuire), and
    Robert Carradine (Sam McGuire)
GUEST STARS: Craig Anton (Mr. Pettus),
    Ashlie Brillault (Kate Sanders),
    Byron Fox (Danny Kessler),
    Clayton Snyder (Ethan Craft)

WHAT HAPPENS?

Lizzie can't wait for the science class field trip, when she'll get to hang out with her friends—and no parents! Then disaster strikes. Her mom becomes the last-minute replacement as a chaperone. Lizzie just knows her mom will embarrass her!

On the trip, Lizzie's science teacher, Mr. Pettus, gives the kids a contest to identify plant species. When the girls lose, they have to dig for earthworms. *Ew!* Then the boys attack the girls with water guns. Could the trip get any worse? Lizzie wonders.

Back home, Matt and Mr. McGuire think they have it made with Lizzie and Mrs. McGuire gone. But when dinner becomes a disaster, they break down and order pizza.

Meanwhile, in the great outdoors, Lizzie's mom helps the girls get back at the boys by leading a midnight toilet paper raid on their tent. When Mr. Pettus walks in on the prank, he only catches Mrs. McGuire, who told the girls to run. Just as he is about to punish all of the girls, Mrs. McGuire tells him she worked alone, sparing the girls from punishment. Everyone thinks Mrs. McGuire is the coolest, and at school on Monday, Lizzie is finally proud of her "cool mom."

DID YOU KNOW?

- In this episode, Ethan Craft and Danny Kessler appear together for the first and only time in the *Lizzie McGuire* series.

> Hey, I guess my mom is kinda cool, after all!

- Lizzie owns a stuffed pig named Mr. Snuggles. Kate once owned a teddy bear named Mr. Stewart Wugglesby.

- Matt and Mr. McGuire use a cookbook called *Cooking for Complete Idiots*.

- According to executive producer Stan Rogow, the creation of the Toon Lizzie installments for each episode took about six weeks.

- After the *Lizzie McGuire* actors *finished* filming, Tape House Toons in New York City *started* their work—on creating the animated Lizzie segments of the show. A crew in New York routinely collaborated on scripts and sent storyboard suggestions back to Hollywood, California, where the show was filmed.

CAN YOU SPOT THE BLOOPERS?

- Miranda says Lizzie has pink ducky pajamas, but when they are shown, the ducks are yellow.

- In the beginning of the episode, Toon Lizzie says the camping trip is forty-eight hours, but it is only overnight.

DIRECTOR: Savage Steve Holland
WRITER: Trish Baker
EXECUTIVE PRODUCERS: Stan Rogow & Susan Estelle Jansen
CONSULTING PRODUCERS: Douglas Tuber & Tim Maile
PRODUCER: Jill Danton
SERIES CREATED BY: Terri Minsky
CAST STARS: Hilary Duff (Lizzie McGuire),
  Lalaine (Miranda Sanchez),
  Adam Lamberg
    (David "Gordo" Gordon),
  Jake Thomas (Matt McGuire),
  Hallie Todd (Jo McGuire), and
  Robert Carradine (Sam McGuire)
GUEST STAR: Craig Anton (Mr. Pettus)

EPISODE NUMBER 6: "JACK OF ALL TRADES"

WHAT HAPPENS?

In science class, Gordo, Miranda, and Lizzie take aptitude tests that suggest their future careers. The tests reveal that Miranda should be a Navy Seal, Lizzie a cosmetologist, and Gordo a blackjack dealer. Gordo is disappointed with his test results, because he already feels like his science teacher doesn't like him. Gordo is one of the smartest kids in school, but Mr. Pettus keeps giving him Bs. Gordo plans to prove Mr. Pettus is biased by convincing Lizzie to turn in his very cool model of the human brain as her project in class. He's so proud of the project that he can't stand it being graded with a B.

Mr. Pettus loves the brain model and gives Lizzie an A+. Then Gordo steps in and says it was his project. While he's going off on Mr. Pettus for being unfair, the brain explodes, getting goo all over Gordo, Mr. Pettus, and Lizzie. Mr. Pettus tells Gordo that he's his best student, and he only gives him Bs to challenge him to do better.

Meanwhile, Matt decides to change his name to "M-Dogg." His parents agree, but only if he'll call them DD and Mu Mu. Matt gives up and goes back to being Matt.

DID YOU KNOW?

- All of the Lizzie McGuire episodes took about the same time to shoot—five days each.

- In this episode, we learn that Lizzie wanted to be a veterinarian when she was a little girl.

- Miranda wants to be a backup singer.

- Matt sleeps on action hero sheets.

- Gordo calls Lizzie and Miranda "Rachel and Monica" a reference to the characters from the TV series *Friends*.

- Miranda and Lizzie took swimming lessons together as children.

> Okay, Gordo, stop being so melodramatic (and deal me in)!

CAN YOU SPOT THE BLOOPERS?

- As Lizzie is about to leave the house, her backpack is unzipped, but in the next shot it's zipped.

- After the brain explodes, a piece of slime appears, disappears, and reappears during the scene where Gordo is talking to Mr. Pettus.

- At dinner, after the brain explosion, Lizzie is wearing the same shirt she wore at school. With all the slime that hit her, shouldn't that shirt be in the washer?!

EPISODE NUMBER 7: "MISADVENTURES IN BABYSITTING"

DIRECTOR: Mark Rosman
WRITERS: David Blum & Stacy Kramer
EXECUTIVE PRODUCERS: Stan Rogow & Susan Estelle Jansen
CONSULTING PRODUCERS: Douglas Tuber & Tim Maile
PRODUCER: Jill Danton
SERIES CREATED BY: Terri Minsky
CAST STARS: Hilary Duff (Lizzie McGuire),
  Lalaine (Miranda Sanchez),
  Adam Lamberg
    (David "Gordo" Gordon),
  Jake Thomas (Matt McGuire),
  Hallie Todd (Jo McGuire), and
  Robert Carradine (Sam McGuire)
GUEST STARS: Diana Weng (Mrs. Shin),
  Ashlie Brillault (Kate Sanders),
  Randy McPherson (Policeman),
  Mike McGaughy (Stunt Double Sam)

WHAT HAPPENS?

Lizzie is *so* over having a babysitter! When the regular sitter cancels, she tries to convince her parents that she's old enough to babysit herself and Matt. They finally say okay, and the next night Lizzie, Miranda, and Gordo team up to babysit Matt. But Matt is a hyperactive brat, and he won't listen to anything Lizzie says. She's so frustrated that she even takes it out on Miranda and Gordo, and they get into a fight.

Meanwhile, out at a restaurant on their date night, Mr. and Mrs. McGuire worry about their kids. Mr. McGuire decides to run home, peek in the window, and make sure everything's okay. But when he gets there, Matt has accidentally knocked out the power and Mr. McGuire gets worried. He tries to get in the house, but the kids think he's a burglar, so they protect the house with pranks. The kids finally call the police, who come to arrest Mr. McGuire. The police ask Lizzie if the "burglar" is her father, and Lizzie hesitates before telling the truth, just to get him back for spying on her. Her parents apologize for not trusting Lizzie and she forgives them.

DID YOU KNOW?

Babysitting? Piece o' cake!

- In this episode, Kate's last name is pronounced "Saunders." In other episodes, such as episode #15 "Night of the Day of the Dead" and episode #25 "Last Year's Model," it is pronounced "Sanders."

- When Lizzie was six, she thought monsters lived in her closet.

- The episode's title is a takeoff of the 1987 movie *Adventures in Babysitting*.

- Actor Robert Carradine, who plays Lizzie's dad, had a stunt double for this episode.

- Gordo has a crush on supermodel Tyra Banks.

- When Toon Lizzie says "I'm queen of the world," she's referring to the movie *Titanic*, whose main character says, "I'm king of the world," while standing on the doomed ship's prow.

CAN YOU SPOT THE BLOOPERS?

- When Gordo walks up to the girls, after turning on the power, there's a blue "X" on the floor where he stops.

- In the first scene, Miranda starts to grin and looks at the camera after saying her line, but the scene stayed in the final cut. Scenes like this would usually end up in the blooper reel.

EPISODE NUMBER 8:
"ELECTION"

DIRECTOR: Brian K. Roberts
WRITER: Melissa Gould
EXECUTIVE PRODUCERS: Stan Rogow & Susan Estelle Jansen
CONSULTING PRODUCERS: Douglas Tuber & Tim Maile
PRODUCER: Jill Danton
SERIES CREATED BY: Terri Minsky
CAST STARS: Hilary Duff (Lizzie McGuire),
  Lalaine (Miranda Sanchez),
  Adam Lamberg
    (David "Gordo" Gordon),
  Jake Thomas (Matt McGuire),
  Hallie Todd (Jo McGuire), and
  Robert Carradine (Sam McGuire)
GUEST STARS: Ashlie Brillault (Kate Sanders),
  Kyle J. Downes (Larry Tudgeman),
  Davida Williams (Claire Miller),
  Sara Paxton (Holly),
  Rachel Snow (Veruca),
  Bernard Kira (Thug),
  Cory Hodges (Protester)

WHAT HAPPENS?

Hillridge Junior High is about to have school elections, and the only candidates are snobby cheerleader Claire and school nerd Larry Tudgeman. Gordo, Miranda, and Lizzie are disappointed that no one "normal" is running for class president, so Gordo convinces Lizzie to run as the "voice of the people."

With Gordo masterminding her campaign, Lizzie gives crowd-pleasing speeches and gets the votes of nearly every club in school, except the ultracool drama club. She decides to act like one of them to get their votes, dressing in black and hanging with them. But soon she's obsessed with them and starts ignoring all the other kids. She even snubs Miranda and Gordo.

On election day, Lizzie is brought down to earth when Larry Tudgeman wins. His campaign promise—to eat a worm for every vote—really paid off. Lizzie apologizes to Miranda and Gordo and they forgive her.

Meanwhile, Matt has been worrying his parents by talking to an imaginary friend, Jasper. When they discover it's all an act, they get even by forcing him to wash an invisible donkey!

DID YOU KNOW?

- Popular student hangout, the Digital Bean cybercafé, makes its debut in this episode.

President Lizzie— I like the sound of that. Does Air Force One serve smoothies?

- Robert Carradine, who plays Lizzie's father, was "the head nerd" in the 1984 feature film comedy, *Revenge of the Nerds.* When Mr. McGuire tells Lizzie he was president of his school's audiovisual club, a picture of him as his character in *Revenge of the Nerds* is shown.

- "The Claire Witch Project" is a reference to the hit horror movie *The Blair Witch Project.*

- Toon Lizzie recites the often-quoted Sally Field Academy Awards speech, in which it is thought she said, "You like me, you really, really like me." But the truth is, Field actually said, "I can't deny the fact that you like me! Right now, you like me!"

- The nerdy kids at school are called the "Dorkestra."

- Sara Paxton, from the movie *Sleepover*, plays the outgoing class president.

CAN YOU SPOT THE BLOOPERS?

- Gordo refers to Larry carrying a "bowl" of worms, but he always carried around a bucket of worms.

- After the election, Lizzie is wearing black sunglasses on her head, but in the next scene at the Digital Bean, they've been replaced with a black headband.

21

EPISODE NUMBER 9:
"I DO, I DON'T"

DIRECTOR: Steve De Jarnatt
WRITERS: Nina G. Bargiel & Jeremy J. Bargiel
EXECUTIVE PRODUCERS: Stan Rogow & Susan Estelle Jansen
CONSULTING PRODUCERS: Douglas Tuber & Tim Maile
PRODUCER: Jill Danton
SERIES CREATED BY: Terri Minsky
CAST STARS: Hilary Duff (Lizzie McGuire),
Lalaine (Miranda Sanchez),
Adam Lamberg
(David "Gordo" Gordon),
Jake Thomas (Matt McGuire),
Hallie Todd (Jo McGuire), and
Robert Carradine (Sam McGuire)
GUEST STARS: Ashlie Brillault (Kate Sanders),
Clayton Snyder (Ethan Craft),
Kyle J. Downes (Larry Tudgeman)
COSTARS: Candy Brown Houston (Mrs. Stebel),
Chelsea J. Wilson (Cop Kid),
Mitchah Williams (Farmer Kid)

WHAT HAPPENS?

In Social Studies class, Lizzie and her classmates are paired up for a mock marriage project. The following week, they are to give presentations about how their marriages went at a fake twenty-year reunion. Popular snob Kate is paired up with geek Larry Tudgeman. Lizzie is just dying to be paired with her crush, Ethan Craft, but she gets Gordo instead. Oh well, she thinks, the project will be a breeze with Gordo as her partner. But she is totally jealous when Miranda gets to be "married" to Ethan!

At their café hangout, the Digital Bean, Lizzie overhears Kate convincing Ethan to dump Miranda at the upcoming presentation. Lizzie is shocked and warns Miranda what Ethan is planning. At the "reunion," Miranda stuns Ethan by leaving him first! Then Larry gets revenge on Kate dumping him by pouring a bowl of punch on her head.

At home, Matt is acting mysterious. Mr. McGuire follows him and discovers his hiding place, the Matt Cave. Mr. McGuire thinks it's awesome and hangs out there, too. Eventually Mrs. McGuire finds the guys and advises them to get out of there before it falls in on them!

DID YOU KNOW?

I'm happy for Miranda . . . really.

- A typical shooting schedule for the young actors was 4½ hours in front of the camera, 3 hours of school, 1 hour of recreation, and 1 hour for lunch. This was their schedule every day, five days a week!

- This is the first episode where Ethan Craft is shown to be Lizzie and Miranda's crush.

- In Miranda and Ethan's "marriage," their kids are named Britney, Gwyneth, and Ethan Jr.

- Gordo's garbage man costume displays the name tag "Tom."

CAN YOU SPOT THE BLOOPERS?

- Gordo says "We've been larried less than a period" instead of "married."

- When the bowl of punch is poured over Kate's head, actress Ashlie Brillault can't help smiling, even though her character Kate would never have found such a thing funny.

- At the end, Lizzie is supposed to say "not taking people for granted," but she says "granite."

EPISODE NUMBER 10: "BAD GIRL MCGUIRE"

DIRECTOR: Anson Williams
WRITER: Melissa Gould
EXECUTIVE PRODUCERS: Stan Rogow & Susan Estelle Jansen
CONSULTING PRODUCERS: Douglas Tuber & Tim Maile
PRODUCER: Jill Danton
SERIES CREATED BY: Terri Minsky
CAST STARS: Hilary Duff (Lizzie McGuire),
Lalaine (Miranda Sanchez),
Adam Lamberg
(David "Gordo" Gordon),
Jake Thomas (Matt McGuire),
Hallie Todd (Jo McGuire), and
Robert Carradine (Sam McGuire)
GUEST STARS: Jackie Angelescu (Angel Lieberman),
Page Leong (Mrs. Wortman)
COSTAR: Daniel Escobar (Mr. Escobar)

WHAT HAPPENS?

In class, Lizzie is bugged by school rebel Angel, who wants to cheat off Lizzie's test. Angel calls Lizzie a coward and puts gum in her hair, so Lizzie lets her cheat. The teacher catches them, however, and they both get detention.

Lizzie can't believe she got detention, but she's surprised to find it isn't so bad, and she and Angel actually become friends. When she gets home, she lies to her mom about where she's been. This sets off a string of Bad Lizzie adventures.

She starts dressing like a rebel and hanging out with Angel, skipping class and forging notes. Miranda and Gordo worry about the new rebel Lizzie and stage an intervention. They sit her down and show her a video they made to remind her that she is a good girl at heart. She realizes Miranda and Gordo are right, so she says good-bye to Angel and goes back to being a good girl.

Meanwhile, Matt has decided he wants more freedom, so his parents agree to let him stay up as late as he wants. He has a blast the first night, but as the days go by, he gets more and more tired. He finally admits that he needs a bedtime, and life goes back to normal.

DID YOU KNOW?

- This episode was voted a Top 5 favorite *Lizzie* episode in a 2004 Disney Online poll. Position number: 3.

- Angel calls the school's dweebs and geeks "Double Es."

- This episode's director, Anson Williams, played Potsie on the popular TV series *Happy Days*.

- On Matt's first late night, he imitates Tom Cruise's famous dance scene from the movie *Risky Business*.

CAN YOU SPOT THE BLOOPERS?

- When Angel is putting gum in Lizzie's hair, Lizzie looks to the side at Miranda, but when the shot is shown from Angel's view, Lizzie is looking straight ahead.

- When Lizzie first enters the detention room, she is carrying a binder with a pink sticker that says "Lizzie." Watch that sticker as she talks to Mr. Escobar—it seems to disappear and reappear.

- In class, at the beginning, Gordo is wearing a long-sleeved T-shirt under his button-up shirt, but in the next scene, he's wearing a short-sleeved T-shirt under his shirt.

EPISODE NUMBER 11: "BETWEEN A ROCK AND A BRA PLACE"

DIRECTOR: Mark Rosman
WRITERS: Nina G. Bargiel & Jeremy J. Bargiel
EXECUTIVE PRODUCERS: Stan Rogow & Susan Estelle Jansen
CONSULTING PRODUCERS: Douglas Tuber & Tim Maile
PRODUCER: Jill Danton
SERIES CREATED BY: Terri Minsky
CAST STARS: Hilary Duff (Lizzie McGuire),
Lalaine (Miranda Sanchez),
Adam Lamberg
(David "Gordo" Gordon),
Jake Thomas (Matt McGuire),
Hallie Todd (Jo McGuire), and
Robert Carradine (Sam McGuire)
SPECIAL GUEST STAR: David Carradine (Himself)
GUEST STARS: Ashlie Brillault (Kate Sanders),
Davida Williams (Claire Miller)
COSTARS: Ty Upshaw (Mr. Coppersmith),
Amelia Marshall (Mrs. Miller),
Dana Pauley (Saleswoman)

WHAT HAPPENS?

Lizzie and Miranda feel like losers when they realize every girl at school wears a bra except them. They try to trick Lizzie's mom into driving them to the mall for "school supplies," but Lizzie's a terrible liar, and she admits they are really going bra shopping. Mrs. McGuire is excited and offers to help. But she ends up embarrassing them instead, so Lizzie angrily tells her mother they can shop for themselves. Hurt, Mrs. McGuire gives them money and goes to the food court to wait.

The girls continue to shop, and they even run into people from school, like Claire and their teacher Mr. Coppersmith. After they realize that they don't know what kind of bra they need, Lizzie and Miranda find Mrs. McGuire and ask her to help them shop after all.

While the girls are out, Matt is busy making his audition tape to be Jet Li's sidekick in a new movie. Gordo is the cameraman, and Mr. McGuire tries to help, but he realizes they need backup. He calls a friend named David. The mysterious David turns out to be a kung fu expert, and he helps Matt win the contest!

DID YOU KNOW?

Ugh. Why are mothers *so* embarrassing?

- The actor who plays David is Robert Carradine's real-life half brother David Carradine. David starred in the popular TV series *Kung Fu*.

- Actor Adam Lamberg, who plays Gordo, has been quoted as naming this episode as his favorite one.

- Miranda has a picture of *American Pie* actor Chris Klein in her locker.

- The Kate and Claire "high-five, hair-flip" combo debuts in this episode.

- There is no blooper reel at the end of this episode. Instead, the beginning of Matt's kung fu audition tape is shown.

- When Gordo is directing Matt's video, he wears a baseball hat, a tribute to film director Steven Spielberg, who famously wears a baseball cap when directing. In episode #17 "Gordo's Video," Gordo is actually referred to as "Spielberg" by Miranda.

CAN YOU SPOT THE BLOOPERS?

- When Gordo is directing Matt's video, he's wearing a shirt over his T-shirt, which disappears only to reappear later.

- In one scene, Lizzie and Miranda close their lockers, but as they stand talking, the doors are seen open again.

EPISODE NUMBER 12: "COME FLY WITH ME"

DIRECTOR: Timothy Busfield
WRITERS: Douglas Tuber & Tim Maile
EXECUTIVE PRODUCERS: Stan Rogow & Susan Estelle Jansen
CONSULTING PRODUCERS: Douglas Tuber & Tim Maile
PRODUCER: Jill Danton
SERIES CREATED BY: Terri Minsky
CAST STARS: Hilary Duff (Lizzie McGuire),
   Lalaine (Miranda Sanchez),
   Adam Lamberg
      (David "Gordo" Gordon),
   Jake Thomas (Matt McGuire),
   Hallie Todd (Jo McGuire), and
   Robert Carradine (Sam McGuire)
GUEST STARS: Ashlie Brillault (Kate Sanders),
   Clayton Snyder (Ethan Craft),
   Christian Copelin (Lanny Onasis)
COSTAR: Bernard Kira (Vince)

WHAT HAPPENS?

Gordo, who prides himself on his unique (and sometimes strange) interests, has a new obsession: music from the "Rat Pack" era. Lizzie and Miranda think it's kind of dorky, but when Ethan grabs a Rat Pack CD from them on the school bus and listens to it, he likes it! Suddenly, the entire school is into the Rat Pack, and Kate begs Lizzie and Miranda to help her with the next school dance. Lizzie and Miranda are psyched to be popular. They go to Gordo for help in choosing music, but he's angry at them for spreading the Rat Pack trend since he considered it his personal passion. Lizzie tries to make him realize that just because other people like something, it doesn't mean he can't. But he's still angry.

Later, at the dance, Gordo walks in, dressed like Rat Pack leader Frank Sinatra, and tells Lizzie and Miranda he's totally sorry he let them down. Happily, they all take a spin on the dance floor.

Meanwhile, Matt and his friend Lanny try to set a world record, but fail at everything they try until Mrs. McGuire tells them they must have set a world record for most failed attempts at a world record!

DID YOU KNOW?

> Just call me a cool, cool cat . . . er, *rat*!

- The "Rat Pack" refers to the name given to a group of entertainers. The group included Frank Sinatra, Dean Martin, Sammy Davis Jr., Peter Lawford, and Joey Bishop. During the 1950s and '60s, the Rat Pack performed famous shows in big Las Vegas casinos.

- This episode's title is also the title of a classic song, sung by Frank Sinatra.

- In this episode, we learn Gordo once had a unicycle and a Zen garden.

- Gordo's middle name is Zephyr (pronounced ZEH-fur).

- The Hillridge Junior High's sports teams are called the Wildcats.

- Lanny makes his first appearance in the series. We learn he only eats pumpkin ice cream. (But check out episode #53 "She Said, He Said, She Said.")

- According to executive producer Stan Rogow, the producers and writers all had so much fun with a character who didn't talk that they decided to make Lanny a semiregular character.

CAN YOU SPOT THE BLOOPERS?

- When Matt and Lanny are flipping through the *Book of World Records*, they stop at the section marked "Computer Technology," but Matt actually reads the words: "World's Largest Pancake."

EPISODE NUMBER 13: "RANDOM ACTS OF MIRANDA"

DIRECTOR: Steve De Jarnatt
WRITERS: Douglas Tuber & Tim Maile
EXECUTIVE PRODUCERS: Stan Rogow & Susan Estelle Jansen
CONSULTING PRODUCERS: Douglas Tuber & Tim Maile
PRODUCER: Jill Danton
SERIES CREATED BY: Terri Minsky
CAST STARS: Hilary Duff (Lizzie McGuire),
Lalaine (Miranda Sanchez),
Adam Lamberg
(David "Gordo" Gordon),
Jake Thomas (Matt McGuire),
Hallie Todd (Jo McGuire), and
Robert Carradine (Sam McGuire)
SPECIAL GUEST STAR: Orlando Brown (Travis Elliot)
GUEST STARS: Daniel Escobar (Mr. Escobar),
Kyle J. Downes (Larry Tudgeman),
Christian Copelin (Lanny Onasis)
COSTARS: Troy Rowland (Mr. Lang),
Mitchah Williams (Father),
Ryan Shannon (Kid)

WHAT HAPPENS?

Lizzie is excited to be a member of the school's newspaper staff. After Miranda lands the lead in the school play, Lizzie decides to review it for the paper. But Miranda is a terrible actress and gives a cringe-worthy performance. Lizzie is torn about her review. She doesn't want to hurt Miranda's feelings, but she finally decides to give an honest review.

The next day, Miranda feels betrayed and tells Lizzie she's just jealous. But after Gordo shows Miranda the video he made of the play, Miranda realizes she really *is* a bad actress. Lizzie has also realized she should have supported Miranda. The girls apologize. But Lizzie becomes worried anew when Miranda joins the glee club. At the school recital a month later, however, Miranda gives a fantastic performance.

Meanwhile, Matt and Lanny want to buy walkie-talkies, but Matt's parents won't give him $90 to buy them. They tell Matt to raise the money as a lesson. Matt has a yard sale, and soon he has his walkie-talkies. But Mr. and Mrs. McGuire discover what Matt sold to get the money—every last thing in his bedroom! No more "lessons" for a while, they decide.

DID YOU KNOW?

The only thing that stinks more than Miranda's acting–is my having to tell her!

- The song Miranda performs in glee club is "Reflection" from the Disney animated film *Mulan*.

- In real life, the actress who plays Miranda, Lalaine, is an accomplished singer. At the age of ten, she had already been cast in a national tour of the famous Broadway musical *Les Miserables*.

- Orlando Brown, star of Disney Channel's *That's So Raven*, appears as Miranda's costar in the school musical.

- In this episode, we learn Gordo played a question mark in his 3rd grade grammar pageant.

- Lanny, who never speaks, belongs to his church's choir. (Hello?!)

CAN YOU SPOT THE BLOOPERS?

- During Miranda's play, seated behind Matt and Lanny, a boy with sunglasses and one with red hair can be seen magically moving to different locations from shot to shot.

EPISODE NUMBER 14: "LIZZIE'S NIGHTMARE"

DIRECTOR: Jace Alexander
WRITER: Melissa Gould
EXECUTIVE PRODUCERS: Stan Rogow & Susan Estelle Jansen
CONSULTING PRODUCERS: Douglas Tuber & Tim Maile
PRODUCER: Jill Danton
SERIES CREATED BY: Terri Minsky
CAST STARS: Hilary Duff (Lizzie McGuire),
Lalaine (Miranda Sanchez),
Adam Lamberg
(David "Gordo" Gordon),
Jake Thomas (Matt McGuire),
Hallie Todd (Jo McGuire), and
Robert Carradine (Sam McGuire)
SPECIAL GUEST STAR: Phill Lewis (Principal)
GUEST STARS: Ashlie Brillault (Kate Sanders),
Clayton Snyder (Ethan Craft),
Christian Copelin (Lanny Onasis)
COSTARS: Tony Jones (Police Officer #1),
Randy McPherson (Police Officer),
Hayk Kalantarian (Hayk)

WHAT HAPPENS?

Lizzie's dream has come true: Ethan Craft wants to have lunch with her! She is on cloud nine that morning, but Matt secretly slips honey on her phone, which totally messes up her hair. Mr. and Mrs. McGuire yell at Matt and ground him. He runs to catch the bus, but accidentally gets on the junior high bus instead. He goes along for the ride and even picks a fight with Ethan over a bus seat. Ethan admires Matt's courage and takes him under his wing.

When Lizzie finally gets to school, she hears all about some new kid who is really cool and has done amazing things—like worked with film director Steven Spielberg. Lizzie is horrified when she discovers the "new kid" is Matt! She does all she can to get him kicked out of school, but no one believes her, not even Principal Tweedy. She finally gets rid of him by calling the police, who take Matt away. But Lizzie's classmates even think that is cool! Ethan finally calls Lizzie that night to ask if she's free on Saturday—he wants her to pick up a pizza so he and Matt can have lunch together. He loves that little guy!

DID YOU KNOW?

Matt has infested my school. Call pest control!

- In this episode, Matt claims he worked with famous director Steven Spielberg. In real life, the actor who plays Matt, Jake Thomas, did work with Spielberg on the movie *A.I. Artificial Intelligence*.

- Matt tells everyone at junior high that his name is Matt Bond, a reference to James Bond, the famous superspy of books and movies.

- A garden gnome, like the one seen in the Lizzie episode "Misadventures in Babysitting," is seen as a lamp in this episode. In later episodes, we learn that Mr. McGuire's hobby is painting garden gnomes (and he even subscribes to the magazine *Modern Gnome*)!

- Miranda has a poster of Christina Aguilera on her wall.

CAN YOU SPOT THE BLOOPERS?

- Kate doesn't recognize Matt, even though she and Lizzie used to be best friends.

- Matt mentions chicken-noodle casserole, and a shot from "When Moms Attack" is shown. But in that episode, the food is tuna-noodle casserole.

- When Lizzie is talking to Miranda and Gordo about the outfit she wore the day before, Lizzie says the green spinach clashes with her red outfit, but in the picture shown, she is wearing yellow.

33

DIRECTOR: Neal Israel
WRITERS: Douglas Tuber & Tim Maile
EXECUTIVE PRODUCERS: Stan Rogow & Susan Estelle Jansen
CONSULTING PRODUCERS: Douglas Tuber & Tim Maile
PRODUCER: Jill Danton
SERIES CREATED BY: Terri Minsky
CAST STARS: Hilary Duff (Lizzie McGuire),
Lalaine (Miranda Sanchez),
Adam Lamberg
(David "Gordo" Gordon),
Jake Thomas (Matt McGuire),
Hallie Todd (Jo McGuire), and
Robert Carradine (Sam McGuire)
GUEST STARS: Ashlie Brillault (Kate Sanders),
Kyle J. Downes (Larry Tudgeman),
Dyana Ortelli (Mrs. Sanchez),
Armando Molina (Mr. Sanchez),
Christian Copelin (Lanny Onasis)
COSTARS: Korben Akira (Big Kid),
Lawrence A. Mandley (Teacher)

WHAT HAPPENS?

It's Halloween—time for treats and *tricks*! At school,
Kate heads the committee for the Halloween dance. Lizzie really
wants to be the dungeon mistress, so she can dress like a hottie
vampire babe. Kate tells Lizzie she can—*if* she cleans out the
janitor's closet. Lizzie does, but Kate makes Lizzie wear a dorky
clown costume instead. Talk about evil!

At the Halloween party, Kate gets all the attention because
she's wearing the hottie vampire outfit. A fuming Lizzie wants
revenge. And she gets it! Before the party started, Miranda's
parents brought traditional Day of the Dead dolls as props. Kate
rudely told Miranda to get rid of them, and Miranda warned Kate
not to anger the spirits.

Now, at the party, Lizzie convinces Kate that the spirits have
turned Matt into dust and trapped Gordo inside a Burger Buddy
toy. Kate starts to freak out. Then Lizzie pretends to become a
zombie and chases Kate. Petrified, Kate follows Miranda's
instructions to get rid of the spirits. First, she pours punch over
her head, then she rubs cake all over herself. Everyone at the
party thinks it's hilarious that Kate got tricked!

34

DID YOU KNOW?

- "Day of the Dead" (*Día de los Muertos*) is an actual Mexican holiday, celebrated during the same season as Halloween. It is a festive time when families remember those members who have died. Families will visit the cemetery and spruce up the grave site, decorating it with flowers then setting out and enjoying a picnic. Grave sites and family altars in homes are decorated with flowers and adorned with religious amulets and with offerings that can include food (like Miranda's tamales!).

- The 1962 song "Monster Mash" plays in this episode.

- Kate's last name is pronounced "Sanders" in this episode. In other episodes, it is pronounced "Saunders."

- Gordo has a crush on Lizzie's cousin Heather.

> Halloween rules! Especially when Kate gets treated to some just desserts!

CAN YOU SPOT THE BLOOPERS?

- Before she turns into a zombie, Lizzie has a purple ring on her left hand, but in a later shot, the ring is on her right hand. In a shot after that, the ring is back on her left hand.

- Even though vampires are supposed to be repelled by crosses, Kate wears a cross necklace when she's playing the part of the hottie vampire. (Of course, that's Kate, isn't it? She totally wouldn't care about the "legend stuff" if the necklace went with the outfit!)

35

EPISODE NUMBER 16:
"OBSESSION"

DIRECTOR: Savage Steve Holland
WRITERS: Nina G. Bargiel & Jeremy J. Bargiel
EXECUTIVE PRODUCERS: Stan Rogow & Susan Estelle Jansen
CONSULTING PRODUCERS: Douglas Tuber & Tim Maile
PRODUCER: Jill Danton
SERIES CREATED BY: Terri Minsky
CAST STARS: Hilary Duff (Lizzie McGuire),
Lalaine (Miranda Sanchez),
Adam Lamberg
(David "Gordo" Gordon),
Jake Thomas (Matt McGuire),
Hallie Todd (Jo McGuire), and
Robert Carradine (Sam McGuire)
GUEST STARS: Kyle J. Downes (Larry Tudgeman),
Sybyl Walker (Miss Moran)
COSTARS: Chelsea J. Wilson (Parker McKenzie),
Lawrence Mandley (Teacher),
Troy Rowland (Mr. Lang)

WHAT HAPPENS?

After Lizzie and Miranda's school food drive is a success, Lizzie throws herself headfirst into ecological issues. In fact, she becomes *obsessed*. She sets out to conserve water, feed the homeless, and she becomes a vegetarian.

While Lizzie is driving her family nuts with her newfound ways, Gordo becomes obsessed with the school Science Olympics. He wants to beat Larry Tudgeman, the reigning champ, so he stays up every night studying and practicing. Matt is also getting carried away at school, as the newest hall monitor. He tickets several classmates and even his teachers and parents. The last straw for Lizzie is when she yells at her teacher for killing trees needlessly to create a test. After she's sent home, her parents help her to realize that there's such a thing as going overboard. Matt gets sent home, too, for taking his hall monitor job too far. After a head-clearing nap, a back-to-normal Lizzie goes to watch Gordo in the Science Olympics. But his obsession loses him the title when he falls asleep in the middle of the race!

DID YOU KNOW?

> Look out, I'm totally gonna save the world! Yep, just me.

○ The blue leather jacket Miranda wears to Lizzie's house is the same jacket Lizzie wore in episode #11 "Between a Rock and a Bra Place" and episode #9 "I Do, I Don't."

○ Parker McKenzie, who hated Lizzie ever since Lizzie sat on her *Titanic* lunch box in the fifth grade, appears in this episode. And she even compliments Lizzie!

○ School nerd Larry Tudgeman always wears the same shirt, a putty-colored polo with a lime green collar.

○ When Matt says "...and don't call me Shirley," he is quoting the 1980 comedy hit movie *Airplane!*

CAN YOU SPOT THE BLOOPERS?

○ When Lizzie wears a burlap dress to school, Miranda doesn't ask about it until the second time she sees her.

○ Lizzie donates her bed to charity, and her parents didn't know. Whoa, how did they not notice a bed and movers leaving their house?!

DIRECTOR: Steve De Jarnatt
WRITER: Kris Lowe
EXECUTIVE PRODUCERS: Stan Rogow & Susan Estelle Jansen
CONSULTING PRODUCERS: Douglas Tuber & Tim Maile
PRODUCER: Jill Danton
SERIES CREATED BY: Terri Minsky
CAST STARS: Hilary Duff (Lizzie McGuire),
Lalaine (Miranda Sanchez),
Adam Lamberg
(David "Gordo" Gordon),
Jake Thomas (Matt McGuire),
Hallie Todd (Jo McGuire), and
Robert Carradine (Sam McGuire)
GUEST STARS: Ashlie Brillault (Kate Sanders),
Davida Williams (Claire Miller),
Daniel Escobar (Mr. Escobar)
COSTARS: Clayton Snyder (Ethan Craft),
Brian Johnson (Huge Football Player),
Jeffrey Meng (Smaller Footbal Player)
UNCREDITED: Haylie Duff (Girl in Audience)

WHAT HAPPENS?

When Gordo accidentally leaves his camcorder in the cafeteria, he tapes Kate telling Claire that she is really a year older than everyone else in her class because she was held back in kindergarten. This gives him a brilliant idea! He hides his camcorder in various spots at school and tapes his classmates' most embarrassing moments. He plans to put all the footage into a movie for an upcoming competition. But when Miranda finds out he taped her telling Lizzie what she really thinks about everyone in school, she wants him to leave out her footage. Gordo refuses and Lizzie is caught in the middle of a war between her two best friends.

When Gordo's film is finally shown, he has blurred everyone's faces and disguised their voices so no one knows who was featured in his video. Miranda is relieved, and so is Kate.

Meanwhile, back at home, Matt wants to be a stuntman, but his parents stop every stunt he tries to do. He finally settles on being a daredevil, but his ultimate trick is spoiled when Mr. McGuire trips into his stunt and becomes the daredevil instead!

DID YOU KNOW?

- When Gordo is hiding his camcorder, the song "Somebody's Watching Me" by Rockwell plays.

Who knew reality TV could get so complicated?

- Haylie Duff, Hilary Duff's older sister, appears as an uncredited extra in this episode. Look for her during the showing of Gordo's video. There's a shot of her sitting and laughing with another blond girl. Haylie is the one on the left.

- Larry Tudgeman's screensaver is a picture of Miranda. (Hmmmm . . . fast-forward to episode #58!)

- Miranda wears the same shirt she wore in "Between a Rock and a Bra Place."

- When Mr. McGuire talks about a cooking show and says "Bam!" he's referring to the famous chef and restaurateur Emeril Lagasse, who stars in his own cable TV cooking show, and often says "Bam!" when adding spices or other ingredients to a dish.

CAN YOU SPOT THE BLOOPERS?

- At lunch, Miranda says she forgot her backpack, but in the previous scene in the hallway, she is wearing it.

- At lunch when Lizzie is shown from afar, there's nothing around her, but in the close-up, a shrub is directly behind her.

- When Mr. McGuire's head goes through the fence, the wood makes a perfect square when it breaks, but when he pulls his head out, the hole is uneven and messy.

EPISODE NUMBER 18:
"HERE COMES AARON CARTER"

DIRECTOR: Savage Steve Holland
WRITERS: Nina G. Bargiel & Jeremy J. Bargiel
EXECUTIVE PRODUCERS: Stan Rogow & Susan Estelle Jansen
CONSULTING PRODUCERS: Douglas Tuber & Tim Maile
PRODUCER: Jill Danton
SERIES CREATED BY: Terri Minsky
CAST STARS: Hilary Duff (Lizzie McGuire),
  Lalaine (Miranda Sanchez),
  Adam Lamberg
    (David "Gordo" Gordon),
  Jake Thomas (Matt McGuire),
  Hallie Todd (Jo McGuire), and
  Robert Carradine (Sam McGuire)
GUEST STARS: Aaron Carter (Himself),
  Brad Grunberg (Security Guard),
  David Alex Rosen (Video Director)
COSTARS: Angela Oh (Aaron Carter's Manager),
  Gregory Hinton (Caterer),
  Rory J. Shoaf (Set P.A.)

WHAT HAPPENS?

Lizzie and Miranda learn that cute singer Aaron Carter is in their town to film a music video, and it becomes their mission to go to the set. Matt, who learns where the shoot is, comes along, too. When they get to the set, they try their hardest to sneak past the strict guard at the gate, but he won't let them in. Then Matt is mistaken for Aaron's stand-in and is rushed on set, leaving Lizzie, Miranda, and Gordo outside.

Meanwhile, Mr. and Mrs. McGuire enter the scene, break the set rules, and end up in "security guard jail." Lizzie, Gordo, and Miranda finally find their way to Aaron's dressing room. Aaron's manager kicks them out, but agrees to take one of them to meet Aaron. Lizzie tell Miranda to go, and she comes back elated. Then Lizzie realizes she left her tape recorder in Aaron's dressing room and goes to get it. Aaron answers the door, gives her the tape recorder and a kiss! Lizzie is even happier when he asks them to be in his video.

DID YOU KNOW?

Ohmigosh, I'm going to meet Aaron Carter!

- Aaron Carter became a real-life friend of Hilary Duff as a result of their working together on this episode.

- This episode was voted a Top 5 favorite *Lizzie* episode in a 2004 Disney Online poll. Position number: 5.

- An alternate title for this episode was "Aaron Carter Is Coming to Town"—a Lizzie-fication of the popular song "Santa Claus Is Coming to Town."

- In this episode, an actress plays Aaron's manager, but his mother, Jane, is his real manager.

- Aaron's video is supposed to be shot at the "Ren-Mar warehouse" in Lizzie's hometown. The writers named this fictional warehouse after the real Ren-Mar Studios in Hollywood, California, where the *Lizzie McGuire* series was filmed.

- Ren-Mar Studios were the first DesiLu Studios, where most of the *I Love Lucy* episodes were filmed.

- When Lizzie, Miranda, and Gordo are sitting outside the warehouse in their elf costumes, look closely. For a moment, they strike a pose of the famous three monkeys who "see no evil, hear no evil, and speak no evil."

CAN YOU SPOT THE BLOOPERS?

- In the opening scene, Lizzie has food spilled all over her. Food is visible on her right shoulder, but when the camera cuts back to her, it's gone.

EPISODE NUMBER 19:
"SIBLING BONDS"

DIRECTOR: Mark Rosman
WRITERS: Douglas Tuber & Tim Maile
EXECUTIVE PRODUCERS: Stan Rogow & Susan Estelle Jansen
CONSULTING PRODUCERS: Douglas Tuber & Tim Maile
PRODUCER: Jill Danton
SERIES CREATED BY: Terri Minsky
CAST STARS: Hilary Duff (Lizzie McGuire),
Lalaine (Miranda Sanchez),
Adam Lamberg
(David "Gordo" Gordon),
Jake Thomas (Matt McGuire),
Hallie Todd (Jo McGuire), and
Robert Carradine (Sam McGuire)
GUEST STARS: Ashlie Brillault (Kate Sanders),
Clayton Snyder (Ethan Craft),
Daniel Escobar (Mr. Escobar)
COSTAR: Paul Robert Langdon (Heywood Biggs)

WHAT HAPPENS?

On the morning of Lizzie's school charity event,
she's baking cookies when her brother, Matt, whose new
interest is magic, handcuffs himself to her. Lizzie's totally annoyed, of
course. But she becomes really angry when Matt can't find the key! It looks
like they'll be spending the day together. What they don't know is that Mrs.
McGuire hid the key to encourage them to "bond"—and Mr. McGuire is in total
agreement!

Lizzie reluctantly heads to the school event with Matt handcuffed to her. She tries
to hide Matt from crush-boy Ethan, but she can't hide from cheer-queen Kate, who
makes fun of her. Matt may not be Lizzie's favorite person at the moment, but when
she sees her little brother bullied by Heywood Biggs, she scares him off. Matt thanks
Lizzie, and she admits she doesn't want anyone picking on her little brother, except
herself, of course!

Later, Matt helps Lizzie by playing a prank on Kate, who falls into the lake.
When Mr. McGuire saves the day by bringing the key, Lizzie is relieved.
Ethan even asks her out for pizza. Just as she's about to say yes,
she sees Heywood bullying Matt again, and she runs to
rescue him instead. Matt may be annoying,
but he *is* her little bro.

DID YOU KNOW?

- Lizzie wears red streaks in her hair when she attends the charity event.

- Talking about Matt, Ethan says he loves that little guy, a reference to the events in episode #14 "Lizzie's Nightmare."

- The charity event scenes in this episode were filmed at Sherman Oaks Castle Park in Sherman Oaks, California, not far from Ren-Mar Studios, where the *Lizzie McGuire* episodes were filmed.

> Is my brother being paid to drive me crazy?

CAN YOU SPOT THE BLOOPERS?

- At the beginning, when Lizzie is "holding Matt upside down," he is clearly doing a handstand.

- When Sam orders a pizza, it is much smaller than the box it came in.

- Sam takes a piece of pizza, but then the pizza is shown with no pieces missing.

- Kate falls backward into the lake, but her stunt double falls forward.

- The stain on Matt's shirt goes from light to dark, instead of dark to light, as it should if his shirt was drying.

EPISODE NUMBER 20:
"GORDO AND
THE GIRL"

DIRECTOR: Kim Friedman
WRITER: Melissa Gould
EXECUTIVE PRODUCERS: Stan Rogow & Susan Estelle Jansen
CONSULTING PRODUCERS: Douglas Tuber & Tim Maile
PRODUCER: Jill Danton
SERIES CREATED BY: Terri Minsky
CAST STARS: Hilary Duff (Lizzie McGuire),
Lalaine (Miranda Sanchez),
Adam Lamberg
(David "Gordo" Gordon),
Jake Thomas (Matt McGuire),
Hallie Todd (Jo McGuire), and
Robert Carradine (Sam McGuire)
SPECIAL GUEST STAR: Kyla Pratt (Brooke Baker)
GUEST STARS: Christian Copelin (Lanny Onasis),
Davida Williams (Claire Miller),
Carlos Alazraqui (Host),
Armando Molina (Edward Sanchez)

WHAT HAPPENS?

Lizzie and Miranda plan a fun movie-marathon evening, but Gordo passes, claiming he has to spend time with his dad. That same night, however, Miranda and Lizzie see Gordo on a date at the Digital Bean with a popular girl named Brooke Baker. Hurt that Gordo lied to her, Lizzie snaps and tells Gordo that Brooke is just using him. Gordo becomes furious with Lizzie.

Later, Lizzie overhears Brooke's friend Claire talking about Brooke's "hot date." Thinking there's no way she could be talking about Gordo, Lizzie and Miranda follow Brooke to a restaurant, expecting to catch her cheating on Gordo. But they find out her date really is with Gordo—and their quick escape sends them into a waiter who drops pasta all over Lizzie. Gordo is embarrassed when he sees them, but the next day he tells Lizzie and Miranda he understands they were just trying to protect him. Gordo breaks up with Brooke anyway because she gets too possessive, asking him to transfer into all of her classes. He just isn't ready for that kind of commitment!

Meanwhile, Mr. McGuire helps Matt with math. Matt is such a quick learner that he turns his newfound skills into a betting ring. But Mrs. McGuire catches on and puts him out of business.

DID YOU KNOW?

- Kyla Pratt, star of Disney's *The Proud Family* (the voice of Penny Proud), is featured in this episode as Gordo's girlfriend, Brooke.

> No way, nuh-uh . . . Gordo *cannot* have a girlfriend!

- This is the first time Claire is featured without her partner-in-crime (and Lizzie's archrival) Kate Sanders.

- The song "Irresistible," sung by Jessica Simpson, plays in the first scene.

- Brooke calls Gordo by his real first name, David. (And, of course, Gordo is rarely called "David" in the series.)

CAN YOU SPOT THE BLOOPERS?

- When talking about kicking over the Social Studies globe, Matt says "accent" instead of "accident."

- When Mr. McGuire is teaching Matt math using gumballs, he says there are ten in each row, but some rows have eleven.

- After Lizzie and Miranda are covered with pasta, the amount of food on Lizzie's face changes from shot to shot.

45

EPISODE NUMBER 21: "RATED AARGH!"

DIRECTOR: Peter Montgomery
WRITER: Trish Baker
EXECUTIVE PRODUCERS: Stan Rogow & Susan Estelle Jansen
CONSULTING PRODUCERS: Douglas Tuber & Tim Maile
PRODUCER: Jill Danton
SERIES CREATED BY: Terri Minsky
CAST STARS: Hilary Duff (Lizzie McGuire),
Lalaine (Miranda Sanchez),
Adam Lamberg
(David "Gordo" Gordon),
Jake Thomas (Matt McGuire),
Hallie Todd (Jo McGuire), and
Robert Carradine (Sam McGuire)
GUEST STARS: Clayton Snyder (Ethan Craft),
Dot-Marie Jones (Coach Kelly),
Kyle J. Downes (Larry Tudgeman)
COSTARS: Mitchah Williams (Kleenex Kid),
DeVaughn W. Nixon (Snackbar Attendant),
David Alex Rosen (Friend),
Yolanda Laverde (Reporter)
UNCREDITED: Jeremy Bargiel (Choking Man)

WHAT HAPPENS?

It's a nightmare. Larry Tudgeman is chosen to be Lizzie's partner for mouth-to-mouth resuscitation practice in CPR class. She's still trying to get over the horror when she, Miranda, and Gordo find out they're the only kids at school who haven't seen the hot new rated-R movie *Vesuvius: The Eruption*. Their parents say they can't go, but Lizzie, Miranda, and Gordo sneak into the theater anyway.

Before the movie starts, the three spot a man choking on a sourball. Lizzie, with CPR lessons fresh on her mind, comes to the rescue, and performs the Heimlich maneuver. Lizzie's a hero and the local news even films a segment on her. Then the kids realize that if their parents see the news, they'll know they've seen the movie they were not allowed to see!

They rush to Lizzie's house to stop her parents from watching the news—not knowing the movie theater already called them to tell them about Lizzie's lifesaving feat. All three kids end up grounded. But Lizzie gets one last night of fun by trying out Matt's new booth for his school carnival: a Velcro wall.

DID YOU KNOW?

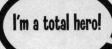

I'm a total hero!

🌼 In this episode, we learn Miranda's full name is Miranda Isabella Sanchez.

🌼 Miranda makes an insider joke when she says, "I don't think I can stand one more talking pig movie." Lalaine, the actress who plays Miranda, once did a voice role in the movie *Babe: Pig in the City*, which is about—you guessed it—a talking pig.

🌼 Jeremy J. Bargiel, who writes many *Lizzie McGuire* episodes, can be seen in this episode playing the part of the choking man in the movie theater. He also shows up in later episodes as a friend of Mr. McGuire's.

🌼 The movie poster for *Vesuvius* identifies it as a "Stan Rogow Film." Stan Rogow is executive producer of *Lizzie McGuire*!

CAN YOU SPOT THE BLOOPERS?

🌼 When Lizzie is talking to the movie ticket guy, her purse strap goes from her shoulder to her elbow then back to her shoulder.

🌼 Right before Lizzie jumps on the Velcro wall, she's wearing sandals, but when she jumps on the wall, she's in white tennis shoes.

**EPISODE NUMBER 22:
"EDUCATING
ETHAN"**

DIRECTOR: Mark Rosman
WRITERS: Nina G. Bargiel & Jeremy J. Bargiel
EXECUTIVE PRODUCERS: Stan Rogow & Susan Estelle Jansen
CONSULTING PRODUCERS: Douglas Tuber & Tim Maile
PRODUCER: Jill Danton
SERIES CREATED BY: Terri Minsky
CAST STARS: Hilary Duff (Lizzie McGuire),
Lalaine (Miranda Sanchez),
Adam Lamberg
(David "Gordo" Gordon),
Jake Thomas (Matt McGuire),
Hallie Todd (Jo McGuire), and
Robert Carradine (Sam McGuire)
GUEST STARS: Clayton Snyder (Ethan Craft),
Arvie Lowe, Jr. (Mr. Dig)
COSTARS: Norma Michaels (Elderly Woman),
Sebastian Jude (Oscar),
Amanda Oshita (Girl),
Katina Waters (Waitress)

WHAT HAPPENS?

Gordo needs to earn money, so Miranda and Lizzie advise him to become a tutor. His first student is the girls' crush-boy, Ethan Craft, who's not going to be easy to teach. Gordo gets annoyed when Miranda and Lizzie try to hang around Gordo and Ethan at the Digital Bean, and he tells the girls they aren't smart enough to be tutors. In a huff, they leave.

The next day, Lizzie offers to help Gordo teach Ethan about fractions because he's just not getting it. Then Ethan asks Lizzie to tutor him instead. She wants to, but she doesn't want to hurt Gordo's feelings, so she says no.

When Ethan fails his next math quiz, Gordo is frustrated and Lizzie finally agrees to tutor Ethan. She teaches him math by using clever Ethan-friendly visual aids—like cheerleaders. With Lizzie's help, Ethan gets a seventy-two on the makeup quiz, and he gives Lizzie a hug. Gordo finally apologizes to Lizzie and Miranda and all is forgiven.

In Matt's world, however, he's bored, so he and his friend become superhero do-gooders—"Matt Man" and "The Incredible Oscar." But when they try to help their neighbors, they just end up making a mess of things.

DID YOU KNOW?

Hello, Ethan? Is anybody in there?

- In this episode, Matt's friend Oscar makes his first appearance in the series.

- Another first: the character of Mr. Dig, Lizzie's favorite substitute teacher, makes the first of many appearances in this episode.

- Lizzie's hair in this episode includes styles with both purple and hot-pink streaks.

- On his first math text, Ethan scores an eleven. (*Yikes!*)

- During one of the scenes when Lizzie is teaching Ethan fractions, you can hear the song "ABC" by the Jackson Five playing.

CAN YOU SPOT THE BLOOPERS?

- Lizzie pronounces the word "stereo" as "steerio."

- When Matt and Oscar are helping the old lady with her grocery bags, they put them on the ground, but in the next shot, she has them in her hands.

EPISODE NUMBER 23:
"LIZZIE STRIKES OUT"

DIRECTOR: Ellen Falcon Gittelsohn
WRITER: Melissa Gould
EXECUTIVE PRODUCERS: Stan Rogow & Susan Estelle Jansen
CONSULTING PRODUCERS: Douglas Tuber & Tim Maile
PRODUCER: Jill Danton
SERIES CREATED BY: Terri Minsky
CAST STARS: Hilary Duff (Lizzie McGuire),
Lalaine (Miranda Sanchez),
Adam Lamberg
(David "Gordo" Gordon),
Jake Thomas (Matt McGuire),
Hallie Todd (Jo McGuire), and
Robert Carradine (Sam McGuire)
GUEST STARS: Clayton Snyder (Ethan Craft),
Arvie Lowe, Jr. (Mr. Dig),
Christian Copelin (Lanny Onasis)
COSTAR: Paul Robert Langdon (Heywood Biggs)

WHAT HAPPENS?

Lizzie is totally psyched when Ethan invites her, Miranda, and Gordo to go bowling that weekend. At home, Mr. McGuire feels like he has no clue about Lizzie's life and asks her out to dinner on Friday night so they can catch up. Lizzie says yes because she thinks bowling with Ethan will be on Saturday. But she finds out that the bowling night is Friday. In a panic, she asks her dad if they can reschedule their dinner. He says okay, but he's obviously hurt. Lizzie feels terrible and talks to her mom, who manages to make her feel totally guilty about letting down her dad!

Meanwhile, Matt and Lanny try to come up with ways to get even with the bully Heywood Biggs. They even try out their "Operation Mummy" trick on Lizzie before trying it on Heywood.

By Friday night, Lizzie decides to go bowling anyway, but she asks her dad to come along too. Problem solved! At the bowling alley, Gordo, who had been struggling the entire week with his secret fear of bowling (which included a past incident where the ball got stuck on his hand), manages to overcome his fear. When he successfully bowls a gutter ball, he jumps for joy.

DID YOU KNOW?

> Hmmm. . . . A night with Ethan or my dad? Thinking, thinking . . .

- Executive Producer Stan Rogow wanted the *Lizzie McGuire* series to really have its own style. Not only did he want to see animation incorporated into each episode, but he also wanted to pioneer an aggressive style of filmmaking for the series. The result: episodes take full advantage of the latest in technology by blending several mediums, including 16 mm film, high-8 video, digital stills, and of course animation, to seamless effect.

- Rogow says he was partly influenced by the 1998 Sundance Film Festival Audience Award-winning German feature film *Run, Lola, Run*. The film's rat-a-tat pace, use of animation and live action, and ever-building momentum inspired the Lizzie producers.

- In this episode, the Wilco Theater, which is showing *Psycho*, is the same theater where the events in episode #21 "Rated Aargh!" take place.

- In this episode, viewers learn that Lizzie's most embarrassing moment was when her pants once split in class!

CAN YOU SPOT THE BLOOPERS?

- When Mr. Dig runs into the tree on his scooter, Miranda calls him "Mr. Digs," adding an "s" to his name.

- After Matt and Lanny fall while wrapping Lizzie up in plastic, Matt's hat falls off, then it's on and off in different shots.

EPISODE NUMBER 24:
"LAST YEAR'S MODEL"

DIRECTOR: Savage Steve Holland
WRITERS: Douglas Tuber & Tim Maile
EXECUTIVE PRODUCERS: Stan Rogow & Susan Estelle Jansen
CONSULTING PRODUCERS: Douglas Tuber & Tim Maile
PRODUCER: Jill Danton
SERIES CREATED BY: Terri Minsky
CAST STARS: Hilary Duff (Lizzie McGuire),
Lalaine (Miranda Sanchez),
Adam Lamberg
(David "Gordo" Gordon),
Jake Thomas (Matt McGuire),
Hallie Todd (Jo McGuire), and
Robert Carradine (Sam McGuire)
GUEST STARS: Ashlie Brillault (Kate Sanders),
Arvie Lowe, Jr. (Mr. Digby Sellers),
Clayton Snyder (Ethan Craft),
Elizabeth Densmore (Jessica),
Christian Copelin (Lanny Onasis)

WHAT HAPPENS?

When *Teen Attitude* magazine advertises a local fashion show, Lizzie tries out and is chosen to be a model. Her debut is a success and Lizzie suddenly becomes a star at school. She's invited to all the popular kids' parties and even Kate Sanders starts sucking up to her. Ethan is acting weird and starstruck, too, and Lizzie starts to wonder what's wrong with everyone. It gets even worse when Gordo and Miranda start acting that way. Lizzie goes to Mr. Dig for advice. He tells her to act like a real diva to teach Gordo and Miranda a lesson.

At her house, Lizzie displays serious attitude. When Gordo and Miranda let her treat them like dirt, she confronts them, saying she wants her real friends back. They come to their senses and agree. At the next fashion show, Lizzie intentionally makes a fool of herself (with a little help from her friends) and is happy to get fired so she can go back to her old normal life.

Meanwhile, Matt uses a gift certificate to buy a hammock. When it breaks, Matt and Lanny employ some creative persuasion to convince the snooty salesman to exchange it.

I'm a star!
I'm a star!

DID YOU KNOW?

- When Matt is shopping in this episode, the song "Shopping" by the Pet Shop Boys plays.

- In this episode, viewers learn that Lanny has a Web site.

- Viewers also learn that Mr. Dig is from East Lansing, Michigan, and his family is originally from Tobago, an island in the Caribbean, and a part of the Republic of Trinidad and Tobago.

- During the first fashion show in the episode, listen for the song "Everybody Wants Ya" by the British pop singing group S Club 7.

- Mr. Dig tells Lizzie he doesn't know who Miranda and Gordo are, but he was just talking to them earlier in the hallway—and he has taught them in the past. (Not a blooper since Mr. Dig does like to play head games with his students!)

CAN YOU SPOT THE BLOOPERS?

- At the country club, when Miranda and Lizzie are in line for drinks, a redheaded girl is standing next to Kate in front of the line, but when the camera pans back to Lizzie and Miranda, the redhead is behind them.

- Check out Lizzie's drink when she's sitting in the hot tub. A flower magically disappears and reappears from shot to shot.

- Watch Lizzie's school locker when she puts her pencil box in it. There seems to be only one book inside. However, after she notices the boy staring at her, several notebooks and textbooks suddenly appear.

EPISODE NUMBER 25:
"THE COURTSHIP OF MIRANDA SANCHEZ"

DIRECTOR: Steve De Jarnatt
WRITER: Melissa Gould
EXECUTIVE PRODUCERS: Stan Rogow & Susan Estelle Jansen
CONSULTING PRODUCERS: Douglas Tuber & Tim Maile
PRODUCER: Jill Danton
SERIES CREATED BY: Terri Minsky
CAST STARS: Hilary Duff (Lizzie McGuire),
Lalaine (Miranda Sanchez),
Adam Lamberg
(David "Gordo" Gordon),
Jake Thomas (Matt McGuire),
Hallie Todd (Jo McGuire), and
Robert Carradine (Sam McGuire)
GUEST STAR: Shan Elliot (Ryan Adams)

WHAT HAPPENS?

After seeing classmate Ryan Adams perform in drama class, Miranda completely falls for the guy. She has only one problem: when he comes anywhere near her, she can't form a complete sentence! Lizzie decides to help. She writes out a script for Miranda to use when she talks to him, and it works. He invites her to lunch.

Since Miranda is still worried about getting tongue-tied, Lizzie hides in a trash can near their lunch table and whispers lines for Miranda to say. But Lizzie falls out of the trash can and Ryan gets freaked out and leaves.

Later, Lizzie talks to Ryan and tries to explain what happened. Ryan jumps to the wrong conclusion, thinking that Lizzie is the one who likes him! He asks Lizzie out and Miranda overhears. Miranda thinks Lizzie is trying to steal her man, but she goes along with Lizzie to meet Ryan at the Digital Bean anyway. At the Digital Bean, Miranda gets to see the real Ryan, and he's not as cool as she thought he was. She realizes that she fell for his acting and not him. Lizzie and Miranda become best friends again.

Meanwhile, Gordo is sick of girl talk, so he starts hanging out with Matt. After a while, though, Gordo gets bored with 24/7 guy stuff and wants to hang out with his best friends again.

DID YOU KNOW?

Love is so confusing!

- Actress Lalaine, who plays Miranda, was nominated for Imagen's Award for Best Supporting Actress in Television for her work on *Lizzie McGuire*. (The Imagen Awards were established in 1985 to encourage and recognize the positive portrayal of Latinos in all media.)

- When Lizzie is walking toward Ryan in the hallway, "I Tried to Rock You But You Only Roll" by Leona Naess plays.

- When Lizzie, Miranda, and Gordo are looking at the stars, "Us Against the World" by Play is heard.

- The basic premise of this episode, in which one character helps another character woo a love interest by providing the right words, was inspired by Edmond Rostand's famous play *Cyrano de Bergerac*, which is set in seventeenth-century France.

CAN YOU SPOT THE BLOOPERS?

- When Lizzie is talking to Ryan in the hallway, a girl in a pink vest passes by. In the next shot, she walks by again—in the same direction.

DIRECTOR: Mark Rosman
WRITERS: Douglas Tuber & Tim Maile
EXECUTIVE PRODUCERS: Stan Rogow & Susan Estelle Jansen
CONSULTING PRODUCERS: Douglas Tuber & Tim Maile
PRODUCER: Jill Danton
SERIES CREATED BY: Terri Minsky
CAST STARS: Hilary Duff (Lizzie McGuire),
Lalaine (Miranda Sanchez),
Adam Lamberg
(David "Gordo" Gordon),
Jake Thomas (Matt McGuire),
Hallie Todd (Jo McGuire), and
Robert Carradine (Sam McGuire)
GUEST STARS: Daniel Escobar (Mr. Escobar),
Ashlie Brillault (Kate Sanders),
Kyle J. Downes (Larry Tudgeman),
Arvie Lowe, Jr. (Mr. Digby Sellers),
Davida Williams (Claire Miller),
Christian Copelin (Lanny Onasis)
COSTARS: Rick Marotta (Rick Marotta),
Ivy Withrow (Violin Girl)

WHAT HAPPENS?

Lizzie, Miranda, and Gordo enter the school's Fact-Athlon, hoping to win a trip to Miami. Their opponents are super-smart Larry Tudgeman, super-snobby Kate Sanders, and Claire Miller. Lizzie and her team have Mr. Dig as their coach. He teaches them in a fun way—they learn math concepts by playing poker, history by playing roles in costume, and lots of other things. While their opponents are stressing about memorizing dates, Lizzie and her team have a blast learning new things in creative ways.

But on the day of the Fact-Athlon, the questions are full of dates and empty statistics. The competition isn't about learning, it's about memorizing! They're slaughtered by the other team. Lizzie, Miranda, and Gordo are disappointed to lose, but when they find out Mr. Dig might quit because of it, they rush to tell him that they did learn a lot, and they're not sorry.

At home, Matt and Lanny's new idea is to start a rock band. They audition several drummers before deciding on Rick Marotta. Their only performance is a hit, but by then, Matt is already over the rock-star thing.

DID YOU KNOW?

- "Facts of Life" was ranked as the number one highest-rated of all the *Lizzie* telecasts. (Ratings were measured among kids ages 6 to 11 on October 12, 2001.)

Learning fun? Who knew?

- In real life, Rick Marotta is an actual professional drummer. He really did play drums with the artists mentioned in the episode (Linda Ronstadt, James Taylor, Steely Dan, John Lennon, and many other artists).

- Matt's furry outfit and sunglasses combo at the performance is modeled after rocker Lenny Kravitz.

- Matt's first choice for his band name is "Spoink."

- Kate gets a red, itchy stress rash during her study mania.

- When Miranda says, "Madonna loves Miami!" Lizzie, Miranda, and Gordo are all pictured with . . . *whoa*, is that really Madonna? Nope, just a look-alike!

CAN YOU SPOT THE BLOOPERS?

- In reading Rick's credits, Matt says, "Linda Ronstand." Her last name is actually "Ronstadt."

- When Lizzie is grabbing things from her locker, they are in her right hand, but in a later shot, they are in her left hand.

EPISODE NUMBER 27:
"THE SCARLET LARRY"

DIRECTOR: Steve De Jarnatt
WRITERS: Amy Engelberg & Wendy Engelberg
EXECUTIVE PRODUCERS: Stan Rogow & Susan Estelle Jansen
CONSULTING PRODUCERS: Douglas Tuber & Tim Maile
PRODUCER: Jill Danton
SERIES CREATED BY: Terri Minsky
CAST STARS: Hilary Duff (Lizzie McGuire),
Lalaine (Miranda Sanchez),
Adam Lamberg
(David "Gordo" Gordon),
Jake Thomas (Matt McGuire),
Hallie Todd (Jo McGuire), and
Robert Carradine (Sam McGuire)
GUEST STARS: Kyle J. Downes (Larry Tudgeman),
Dot-Marie Jones (Coach Kelly),
Ashlie Brillault (Kate Sanders),
Clayton Snyder (Ethan Craft),
Larry Nicholas (Stunt Coordinator),
Clay Cullen (Stunt Double),
Jaimie Ryan (Maintenance #1),
Kevin Jackson (Maintenance #2),
Shawn Lane (Maintenance #3),
Josh Kemble (Maintenance #4),
Julie Adair (Cheerleader #1),
Nancy Thurston (Cheerleader #2)

WHAT HAPPENS?

Lizzie is excited to find out someone has a crush on her, but she's horrified to find out that it's Larry Tudgeman. He asks her out and Lizzie, who is too nice to break his heart, finally agrees. She's surprised when he shows up for the date in his "weekend shirt" and looking kinda cute. He takes her to the science museum and she has a good time.

The next day at school, though, Larry tells everyone that Lizzie is his girlfriend. It's really embarrassing when Kate finds out and blabs it over the loudspeaker. Later that day, Lizzie tries to break things off, saying she doesn't think they're right for each other. To her shock, Larry agrees but tells Lizzie she's the nicest person he knows.

At home, Mrs. McGuire tries to get Mr. McGuire and Matt to clean up all of their junk. They find Mr. McGuire's old soapbox racer and fix it up, but before Matt can launch a successful racing career, Mr. McGuire accidentally crashes it.

DID YOU KNOW?

Okay, people! Larry is sooo not my boyfriend!

🌸 This is the first time Larry wears a shirt other than his regular putty-colored shirt with the lime-green collar. He's dressed up in a black "weekend shirt" for his date with Lizzie.

🌸 In gym class, everyone is wearing their blue T-shirt the same way, except Kate, who's tied her shirt to show off her midriff.

🌸 When Lizzie is at school with her new "boyfriend," the Backstreet Boys song "Get Another Boyfriend" plays.

🌸 When Mr. McGuire terrorizes students in his old soapbox racer, check out two of the cheerleaders. The actresses playing them are Julie Adair, who was Hilary Duff's stunt double in episode #45 "Those Freaky McGuires," and Nancy Thurston, who was her stunt double in episode #21 "Rated Aargh!" and episode #60 "Lizzie's Eleven."

CAN YOU SPOT THE BLOOPERS?

🌸 When Lizzie finds out someone has a crush on her, Toon Lizzie says she's usually the "crushee not the crusher." That's not quite right when you think about it. In reality, she's usually the crusher, not the crushee!

🌸 When Lizzie is square dancing, Ethan is in her group, and everyone but him hears Lizzie speculate that he's the one crushin' on her. How did he not hear her say that, too? Hmmmm . . .

DIRECTOR: Anson Williams

WRITERS: Nina G. Bargiel & Jeremy J. Bargiel

EXECUTIVE PRODUCERS: Stan Rogow & Susan Estelle Jansen

CONSULTING PRODUCERS: Douglas Tuber & Tim Maile

PRODUCER: Jill Danton

SERIES CREATED BY: Terri Minsky

CAST STARS: Hilary Duff (Lizzie McGuire),
Lalaine (Miranda Sanchez),
Adam Lamberg
(David "Gordo" Gordon),
Jake Thomas (Matt McGuire),
Hallie Todd (Jo McGuire), and
Robert Carradine (Sam McGuire)

GUEST STARS: Sean Hogan (Stan Jansen),
Carly Schroeder (Melina Bianco),
Ashlie Brillault (Kate Sanders),
Kyle J. Downes (Larry Tudgeman),
Clayton Snyder (Ethan Craft)

EPISODE NUMBER 28: "THE UNTITLED STAN JANSEN PROJECT"

WHAT HAPPENS?

Director Stan Jansen is at Hillridge Junior High to make a documentary, and he becomes intrigued by Gordo's attitude, especially when he bad-mouths other students. He asks Gordo to be the subject of the documentary, and Gordo isn't sure. But when Stan tells Gordo it will help him become a director, he agrees.

Stan convinces Gordo to stir up trouble by telling off Kate and insulting Ethan and Larry. Gordo even gets Miranda and Lizzie to tell each other's secrets on camera. The girls get mad at each other before realizing it was Gordo's fault. Gordo admits that he's annoyed by Stan and he wishes that Stan would leave him alone. At the Digital Bean, the kids play a trick on Stan to get back at him.

Meanwhile, at Matt's school, his new friend Melina is so good at being a troublemaker that she gets Matt blamed for her antics. He thinks he's the king of pranks, but she always seems to outsmart him. He knows he should be mad at Melina, but he can't help admiring the girl for her great work!

DID YOU KNOW?

Gordo and Miranda, stop fighting and chill! . . . Please?

- Stan Jansen comes from a combination of names taken from the actual Lizzie McGuire executive producers: Stan Rogow and Susan Estelle Jansen.

- Miranda reveals a deep dark secret to Gordo: Lizzie had a crush on him in fourth grade.

- In this episode, viewers learn that Mr. McGuire likes to paint lawn gnomes as a hobby.

- Blondie's "One Way or Another" plays when Matt and Melina are playing tricks on each other.

- Melina is an unusual name—but it makes sense when you combine the first names of two of *Lizzie McGuire*'s writers (Melissa Gould and Nina Bargiel)!

CAN YOU SPOT THE BLOOPERS?

- When Larry is yelling at Gordo, he's obviously about to laugh.

- When Gordo writes "Go Away" on his notebook and holds it up, the same words can be seen written on the previous page on the back. It's from either a practice run or an earlier shot.

- When Stan is filming Lizzie, Miranda, and Gordo talking, the same extras keep walking past.

DIRECTOR: Savage Steve Holland
WRITERS: Douglas Tuber & Tim Maile
EXECUTIVE PRODUCERS: Stan Rogow & Susan Estelle Jansen
CONSULTING PRODUCERS: Douglas Tuber & Tim Maile
PRODUCER: Jill Danton
SERIES CREATED BY: Terri Minsky
CAST STARS: Hilary Duff (Lizzie McGuire),
Lalaine (Miranda Sanchez),
Adam Lamberg
(David "Gordo" Gordon),
Jake Thomas (Matt McGuire),
Hallie Todd (Jo McGuire), and
Robert Carradine (Sam McGuire)
GUEST STARS: Kyle J. Downes (Larry Tudgeman),
Dyana Ortelli (Daniella Sanchez),
Armando Molina (Edward Sanchez)

WHAT HAPPENS?

Lizzie gets the ultra-dorky role-playing game Dwarflord as a gift from Gammy McGuire. Her mom convinces her to play it at least once to see if she likes it before giving it away. Lizzie and Miranda think it's lame, but Gordo thinks it's cool. Soon, Gordo is obsessed with Dwarflord and joins a Dwarflord club at school, led by Larry Tudgeman. Gordo gets so into the game and its complex rules that he starts staying up all night and shrugs off studying. After he gets an F on a test, Lizzie and Miranda get seriously worried. They try to talk sense into him, but he won't listen.

Finally, Lizzie and Miranda hatch a plan to get their friend back. Along with Matt, they stage an intervention and show him a homemade video that helps him get over his addiction to Dwarflord. The intervention works and Gordo goes back to being his old self.

Meanwhile, Matt's school project is to observe wildlife. He and his dad climb up a backyard tree to watch a bird's nest, but Matt gets bored soon and quits. Sam and Miranda's father, Mr. Sanchez, end up becoming obsessed with watching the nest and spend days in the tree until the eggs hatch.

DID YOU KNOW?

- When Lizzie tells Gordo "Have fun storming the castle," she quotes the 1987 movie *The Princess Bride*.

Listen carefully, Gordo: put down the dwarf cards and step *away* from the game board.

- The hilarious "video" intervention Lizzie and Miranda stage for Gordo is an intentional imitation of the intervention staged by Miranda and Gordo for Lizzie in the episode titled "Bad Girl McGuire."

- As viewers have learned before, Gammy McGuire sends Lizzie and Matt gifts several times a year because she can never remember their actual birthdays.

CAN YOU SPOT THE BLOOPERS?

- When Matt talks about the time Gordo helped him get his head out of the banister, the poles where his head was stuck are much closer together than the rest of the poles.

- In the hallway, an extra in a red sweater passes the actors multiple times in the same scene.

- When Lizzie and Miranda find out Gordo got an F, an extra in an orange shirt walks up the stairs, and in the next shot, he walks up the stairs again.

63

EPISODE NUMBER 30:
"GORDO'S BAR MITZVAH"

DIRECTOR: Anson Williams
WRITER: Melissa Gould
EXECUTIVE PRODUCERS: Stan Rogow & Susan Estelle Jansen
CONSULTING PRODUCERS: Douglas Tuber & Tim Maile
PRODUCER: Jill Danton
SERIES CREATED BY: Terri Minsky
CAST STARS: Hilary Duff (Lizzie McGuire),
Lalaine (Miranda Sanchez),
Adam Lamberg
(David "Gordo" Gordon),
Jake Thomas (Matt McGuire),
Hallie Todd (Jo McGuire), and
Robert Carradine (Sam McGuire)
GUEST STARS: Michael Mantell (Howard Gordon),
Alison Martin (Roberta Gordon),
Kyle J. Downes (Larry Tudgeman),
Clayton Snyder (Ethan Craft),
Armando Molina (Edward Sanchez),
Dyana Ortelli (Daniella Sanchez),
Pat Crawford Brown (Mrs. Robinson),
Mickey Jones (Biker Guy)
COSTARS: Frank Sotonoma Salsedo
(Native American Guy),
David Alex Rosen (David Rosen),
Jeremy Bargiel (Jeremy Bargiel)

WHAT HAPPENS?

It's Ethan's fourteenth birthday and he gets a new dirt bike, the tradition in his family when someone "becomes a man." Even Larry Tudgeman has to shave, and Gordo wonders when he'll become a man. He wonders if he missed the boat by skipping out on his Bar Mitzvah, the Jewish ceremony where a boy becomes a man on his thirteenth birthday. Gordo decides to videotape several men in the neighborhood, including Mr. McGuire, talking about the day they knew they became a man. After thinking about it for a few days, Gordo decides that he wants to have a Bar Mitzvah after all. Everyone gathers to watch the ceremony and celebrate with Gordo.

Meanwhile, Mrs. McGuire has gone on strike as a mom and leaves Mr. McGuire in charge of disciplining Matt. Soon, the plan backfires when Mr. McGuire starts over-punishing Matt, by disciplining him even when he makes an honest mistake. Mrs. McGuire knows it's time to be in charge again when even Matt asks her to stop striking and be his disciplinarian mother again!

(Pilot Episode) Pool Party

Picture Day

Rumors

I've Got Rhythmic

When Moms Attack

Jack of All Trades

Misadventures in Babysitting

Election

EPISODE 17

Gordo's Video

EPISODE 18

Here Comes Aaron Carter

EPISODE 19

Sibling Bonds

EPISODE 20

Gordo and the Girl

EPISODE 21

Rated Aargh!

EPISODE 22

Educating Ethan

EPISODE 23

Lizzie Strikes Out

EPISODE 24

Last Year's Model

EPISODE 25 The Courtship of Miranda Sanchez

EPISODE 26 Facts of Life

EPISODE 27 The Scarlet Larry

EPISODE 28 The Untitled Stan Jansen Project

David Gordon became a man: TODAY

EPISODE 29 Gordo and the Magic Dwarves

EPISODE 30 Gordo's Bar Mitzvah

EPISODE 31 Lizzie and Kate's Excellent Adventure

EPISODE 32 Just Like Lizzie

EPISODE 33 — Movin' On Up

EPISODE 34 — First Kiss

EPISODE 35 — *El Oro de Montezuma*

EPISODE 36 — Mom's Best Friend

EPISODE 37 — The Rise and Fall of the Kate Empire

EPISODE 38 — Over the Hill

EPISODE 39 — Inner Beauty

EPISODE 40 — Party Over Here

EPISODE 41

Working Girl

EPISODE 42

And the Winner Is

EPISODE 43

In Miranda Lizzie Does Not Trust

EPISODE 44

The Longest Yard

EPISODE 45

Those Freaky McGuires

EPISODE 46

A Gordo Story

EPISODE 47

You're a Good Man, Lizzie McGuire

EPISODE 48

Best Dressed for Much Less

EPISODE 49

Just Friends

EPISODE 50

Grubby Longjohn's Olde Tyme Revue

EPISODE 51

Bunkies

EPISODE 52

Lizzie's and Miranda's Magic Train

EPISODE 53

She Said, He Said, She Said

EPISODE 54

Lizzie in the Middle

EPISODE 55

The Greatest Crush of All

EPISODE 56

One of the Guys

EPISODE 57 Grand Ole Grandma

EPISODE 58 My Fair Larry

EPISODE 59 My Dinner with Dig

EPISODE 60 Lizzie's Eleven

EPISODE 61 Dear Lizzie

EPISODE 62 The Gordo Shuffle

EPISODE 63 Clue-Less

EPISODE 64 Xtreme Xmas

EPISODE 65 Bye, Bye Hillridge Junior High

DID YOU KNOW?

- Songs heard during this episode include "When I Grow Up (To Be a Man)" by the Beach Boys and "Bad Boys" by Inner Circle.

- This is the first time in the *Lizzie McGuire* TV series that Gordo's parents are featured.

Who knew guys were so complicated?

CAN YOU SPOT THE BLOOPERS?

- After dinner at Gordo's house, he and his parents put plates full of food in the sink.

DIRECTOR: Savage Steve Holland

WRITERS: Nina G. Bargiel & Jeremy J. Bargiel

EXECUTIVE PRODUCERS: Stan Rogow & Susan Estelle Jansen

CONSULTING PRODUCERS: Douglas Tuber & Tim Maile

PRODUCER: Jill Danton

SERIES CREATED BY: Terri Minsky

CAST STARS: Hilary Duff (Lizzie McGuire), Lalaine (Miranda Sanchez), Adam Lamberg (David "Gordo" Gordon), Jake Thomas (Matt McGuire), Hallie Todd (Jo McGuire), and Robert Carradine (Sam McGuire)

GUEST STARS: Ashlie Brillault (Kate Sanders), Davida Williams (Claire Miller)

EPISODE NUMBER 31: "LIZZIE AND KATE'S EXCELLENT ADVENTURE"

WHAT HAPPENS?

Both Lizzie and Kate are out sick when everyone in their Social Studies class chooses partners for a project. After school, Miranda and Gordo tell Lizzie that she is partnered with Kate. Lizzie freaks out. Kate isn't happy either, but she agrees to come by Lizzie's house to work on the project, which is a presentation about the country Latvia.

As Lizzie and Kate work together, they talk about old times and start to have fun. Lizzie can't believe she actually had a good time with Kate. After school the next day, Lizzie and Kate go to the Digital Bean to work on their project. They're doing fine until Kate's friends and Lizzie's friends arrive and start arguing with each other.

Meanwhile, Matt believes he's psychic, so he opens a psychic booth in the backyard. He's making a profit until Mrs. McGuire puts an end to his psychic days.

Back at Hillridge Junior High, Lizzie and Kate's project presentation goes well. After class, however, Kate's snotty friends push Kate back into her snotty attitude. And Lizzie's friends push her into dismissing Kate. So, for the sake of their friends, Lizzie and Kate are back to *not* being friends. But when their friends aren't looking, the two girls share one last secret smile.

DID YOU KNOW?

Wait, Kate is actually being . . . normal.

- This episode's title "Lizzie and Kate's Excellent Adventure," is a tribute to the 1989 Keanu Reeves movie *Bill & Ted's Excellent Adventure.*

- This episode was voted a Top 5 favorite *Lizzie* episode in a 2004 Disney Online poll. Position number: 4.

- In the last scene, Jessica Andrews's song "Who I Am" plays.

- This is the last episode of Season One—and the last episode in which Lizzie is in seventh grade.

CAN YOU SPOT THE BLOOPERS?

- When Lizzie screams into her locker, her hand is on the door, but from the interior shot, it's on the bottom of the locker. The next shot from the outside shows her hand on the door again.

- Claire Miller's partner is Ethan Craft, but on presentation day, he's not shown in class.

- When Lizzie and Kate slip while baking, the flour bag falls on the floor, but the flour falls on their heads from above.

EPISODE NUMBER 32:
"JUST LIKE LIZZIE"

DIRECTOR: Anson Williams
WRITER: Melissa Gould
EXECUTIVE PRODUCERS: Stan Rogow & Susan Estelle Jansen
CONSULTING PRODUCERS: Douglas Tuber & Tim Maile
PRODUCER: Jill Danton
SERIES CREATED BY: Terri Minsky
CAST STARS: Hilary Duff (Lizzie McGuire),
Lalaine (Miranda Sanchez),
Adam Lamberg
(David "Gordo" Gordon),
Jake Thomas (Matt McGuire),
Hallie Todd (Jo McGuire), and
Robert Carradine (Sam McGuire)
GUEST STARS: Amy Castle (Andie Robinson),
Ashlie Brillault (Kate Sanders),
Clayton Snyder (Ethan Craft)
COSTARS: Kenny Lao (Busboy),
Aggi Ghidoni (Kid)

WHAT HAPPENS?

Now that Lizzie is in eighth grade, she couldn't be happier. In fact, she takes a seventh grader named Andie under her wing. Andie is thrilled to have Lizzie as a mentor and she's always there to compliment Lizzie. Things start to get weird, though, when Andie starts dressing like Lizzie and even dyes her hair blond! When people at school start mistakenly calling Lizzie "Andie," it's gone way too far. Lizzie even has nightmares of Andie taking over her life, and stealing Ethan Craft!

Lizzie tries to tell Andie nicely to stop mimicking her, but Andie won't listen. Lizzie finally tells Andie to get her own life. Andie gets very upset and leaves. Miranda and Gordo think Lizzie was way too hard on Andie, but the next day at school, Andie has a new mentor: Kate! They all agree that two Lizzies were way cooler than two Kates.

Meanwhile, Matt tries out different methods of earning a merit patch in the Wilderness Cadets, but he always ends up injuring his dad. Finally, Mrs. McGuire realizes Matt has earned the First Aid patch for mending Mr. McGuire.

DID YOU KNOW?

- Costume designer Cathryn Wagner lists this episode as one her top three favorites. "When a classmate copies Lizzie's clothes, it's every girl's nightmare! I had to find clothing that looked good on both girls, and also things that were super-recognizable (not just jeans and a white T-shirt). I'm not sure how Andie knew what Lizzie was wearing each day, but I guess that's the fun of television!"

- Lizzie calls seventh graders "sevies"—but Miranda and Gordo don't know what she's talking about until she explains the term.

- When Lizzie is having nightmares about Andie, the song "I Wanna Be Like You" by Big Bad Voodoo Daddy plays.

CAN YOU SPOT THE BLOOPERS?

- When Lizzie and Andie are talking near the wall of lockers, Lizzie's locker is open in one shot, closed in the next, then open again.

- Andie references Gordo's video from the year before, but if she wasn't in junior high then, how did she know about it? Hmmm ... could be the rumor of the video was spread far and wide beyond the school.

EPISODE NUMBER 33:
"MOVIN' ON UP"

DIRECTOR: Mark Rosman
WRITERS: Nina G. Bargiel & Jeremy J. Bargiel
EXECUTIVE PRODUCERS: Stan Rogow & Susan Estelle Jansen
CONSULTING PRODUCERS: Douglas Tuber & Tim Maile
PRODUCER: Jill Danton
SERIES CREATED BY: Terri Minsky
CAST STARS: Hilary Duff (Lizzie McGuire),
Lalaine (Miranda Sanchez),
Adam Lamberg
(David "Gordo" Gordon),
Jake Thomas (Matt McGuire),
Hallie Todd (Jo McGuire), and
Robert Carradine (Sam McGuire)
GUEST STAR: Christian Copelin (Lanny Onasis)
COSTARS: Vanessa Sapien (Wheelchair Student),
Joy Lauren (Cheerleader),
Willie Green (Student)

WHAT HAPPENS?

At school, Gordo is called into the principal's office. Everyone wonders what's going on, and then Gordo tells Lizzie and Miranda that he can skip eighth grade and go straight to high school. He decides to try it out, and even though Lizzie and Miranda don't want him to go, they agree to support his decision.

On his first day of high school, Gordo feels shorter than everyone and he's even tricked into buying a bogus elevator pass. He's miserable, but when Lizzie meets him at the bus stop, he tells her that he likes high school. She's bugged, but she won't tell him that she wants him to come back to junior high. At her house that night, Lizzie vents to Miranda about how upset she is over Gordo. The girls are surprised when Gordo drops by and tells them he's coming back to junior high. Lizzie is thrilled, but she wants to hear Gordo say he missed them. When she tells Gordo she missed him, he finally tells her he missed her, too.

Meanwhile, Matt and Lanny try out for the elementary school's cheerleading squad. They perform a top-notch cheer and the cheerleaders love it. When they're told only one of them can make the squad, they both refuse, saying they are an unbreakable team.

DID YOU KNOW?

🌸 R.E.M.'s "Everybody Hurts" plays when Gordo is shown at high school.

🌸 When Miranda starts talking about all the grown-up stuff high schoolers do, Gordo references the WB drama, *Dawson's Creek*.

🌸 When Mr. McGuire is teaching Matt to be a man, the song "Macho Man" by the Village People plays.

🌸 The year this episode first aired (2002), Disney Channel's *Lizzie McGuire* was voted "Favorite Television Show" at the 15th Annual Nickelodeon Kids Choice Awards. (It would also win this award a second time in 2003!)

> 8th grade without Gordo? I can't do it!

CAN YOU SPOT THE BLOOPERS?

🌸 When Gordo is talking to a girl in high school he's wearing a brown shirt over a beige shirt, but in every other scene, the beige shirt is over the brown shirt.

🌸 In the blooper reel, Robert Carradine, who plays Mr. McGuire, accidentally calls Matt "Jake." Jake Thomas is the actor who plays Matt!

DIRECTOR: Steve De Jarnatt
WRITER: Terri Minsky
EXECUTIVE PRODUCERS: Stan Rogow & Susan Estelle Jansen
CONSULTING PRODUCERS: Douglas Tuber & Tim Maile
PRODUCER: Jill Danton
SERIES CREATED BY: Terri Minsky
CAST STARS: Hilary Duff (Lizzie McGuire),
Lalaine (Miranda Sanchez),
Adam Lamberg
(David "Gordo" Gordon),
Jake Thomas (Matt McGuire),
Hallie Todd (Jo McGuire), and
Robert Carradine (Sam McGuire)
GUEST STARS: Joe Rokicki (Ronny Jacobs),
Carly Schroeder (Melina)

EPISODE NUMBER 34: "FIRST KISS"

WHAT HAPPENS?

Valentine's Day is almost here and Lizzie feels left out because every girl at school seems to have a boyfriend except her. That is, until she finds out that the McGuire paperboy, Ronny, has a crush on her! She starts hanging out with Ronny and is soon obsessed with him, talking about him 24/7.

When Miranda confronts Lizzie about her annoying behavior, Lizzie tells Miranda she's just jealous. Miranda is hurt and angry and stops talking to Lizzie. Gordo is also bothered by the Ronny situation, but he's not sure why he cares so much. Then Ronny gives Lizzie a friendship ring and her first kiss, and Gordo is stunned when he sees them kissing.

Not long after that, however, Ronny tells Lizzie there's a girl at his school he likes, so he wants to break up. Lizzie is heartbroken and sits crying in the library the next day. She tells Gordo what happened and says Ronny's new girlfriend is probably prettier and more fun than she is. Gordo tells her no one is prettier or more fun than she is. It's exactly what Lizzie needed to hear. She dries her eyes and makes up with Miranda, too.

Meanwhile, Matt is on a quest to complete his baseball card collection, and Melina has the card he wants. He does all her chores, but she doesn't give up her card until he trades her what she demands: Mr. McGuire's entire baseball card collection!

DID YOU KNOW?

- All-time number one favorite! This episode was voted a Top 5 favorite *Lizzie* episode in a 2004 Disney Online poll. Position number: 1!

I'm in love! Sigh.

- Actress Hilary Duff, who plays Lizzie, has said this is her favorite episode.

- Lizzie's boyfriend, Ronny Jacobs, goes to Jefferson Middle School and not Hillridge Junior High.

- The Michelle Branch song "Everywhere" plays when Lizzie and Ronny are dating.

- Lizzie's regular purple cordless phone is replaced with a red phone in this episode.

- This is the first episode where Gordo's crush on Lizzie becomes apparent to viewers.

CAN YOU SPOT THE BLOOPERS?

- When Mr. and Mrs. McGuire are putting away dishes, a light blue plate suddenly becomes dark blue in the next shot.

- Matt is making freshly baked brownies for Melina and tells his parents they are out of vanilla, but he is baking from a box of brownie mix. Vanilla and flour (which is also on the counter) aren't necessary in packaged brownie mix.

DIRECTOR: Savage Steve Holland

WRITERS: Douglas Tuber & Tim Maile

EXECUTIVE PRODUCERS: Stan Rogow & Susan Estelle Jansen

CONSULTING PRODUCERS: Douglas Tuber & Tim Maile

PRODUCER: Jill Danton

SERIES CREATED BY: Terri Minsky

CAST STARS: Hilary Duff (Lizzie McGuire),
Lalaine (Miranda Sanchez),
Adam Lamberg
  (David "Gordo" Gordon),
Jake Thomas (Matt McGuire),
Hallie Todd (Jo McGuire), and
Robert Carradine (Sam McGuire)

SPECIAL GUEST STAR: Erik Estrada (Alejandro)

GUEST STARS: Shalim (Carlos),
Christian Copelin (Lanny Onasis),
Kyle J. Downes (Larry Tudgeman),
Arvie Lowe, Jr. (Mr. Dig)

COSTARS: Peter Leal (Montezuma),
Raja Fenske (Li Tarak),
Maria Beck (Zuzu)

WHAT HAPPENS?

At school, a new foreign exchange student from Indonesia has joined Lizzie's class. She tries to talk to him, but he doesn't understand her. The same day, Lizzie's teacher, Mr. Dig, assigns a paper on a foreign culture to his students.

After school, Miranda tells Lizzie and Gordo that her cousin Carlos, from Mexico, is coming to visit because he's going to compete on a Mexican game show they all enjoy, *El Oro de Montezuma*. When Carlos's teammates can't make it to the show, Lizzie, Gordo, and Miranda agree to be his team. Miranda and Gordo worry about the language barrier, but Lizzie is more concerned about the stunts. After all, Carlos will translate for them. But during the show, Carlos is separated from the group, and they have to fend for themselves. Realizing they have no idea what they're doing, they start a food fight with rice pudding.

For her class project, Lizzie writes a paper about Indonesian culture, because she finally knows what it's like to be in a foreign place and not know the language.

Meanwhile, Matt and Lanny play extreme hide-and-seek.

DID YOU KNOW?

Okay, I'm totally confused. Maybe if I smile and nod a lot?

- When Matt and Lanny are playing hide-and-seek, Duran Duran's "Hungry Like the Wolf" plays.

- Erik Estrada, who plays the game show host Alejandro, starred in the 1970s TV show *CHiPs*.

- In this episode, viewers learn that Mrs. McGuire is from Walla Walla, Washington, and Mr. McGuire is from Kalamazoo, Michigan.

- "*El Oro de Montezuma*" translates to "Montezuma's Gold."

- An alternate title for this episode was "*El Oro del Diablo*," which translates to "The Devil's Gold."

CAN YOU SPOT THE BLOOPERS?

- When Lizzie, Gordo, and Miranda are watching the game show in the beginning of the episode, the potato-chip bowl is filled to the brim, even though they'd all been eating chips.

- Mr. Dig introduces himself as Mr. *Digs*—with an "s."

- When the kids throw rice pudding at Montezuma, there are already stains on his shirt from previous takes of the same scene.

EPISODE NUMBER 36: "MOM'S BEST FRIEND"

DIRECTOR: Steve De Jarnatt
WRITERS: Douglas Tuber & Tim Maile
EXECUTIVE PRODUCERS: Stan Rogow & Susan Estelle Jansen
CONSULTING PRODUCERS: Douglas Tuber & Tim Maile
PRODUCER: Jill Danton
SERIES CREATED BY: Terri Minsky
CAST STARS: Hilary Duff (Lizzie McGuire),
Lalaine (Miranda Sanchez),
Adam Lamberg
(David "Gordo" Gordon),
Jake Thomas (Matt McGuire),
Hallie Todd (Jo McGuire), and
Robert Carradine (Sam McGuire)
SPECIAL GUEST STAR: Michael Mantell (Mr. Gordon)
GUEST STARS: Christian Copelin (Lanny Onasis),
Arvie Lowe, Jr. (Mr. Dig),
Dyana Ortelli (Daniella Sanchez)
COSTARS: Jeremy Bargiel (Bleacher Boy),
David Alex Rosen (Bleacher Boy)

WHAT HAPPENS?

At school, Lizzie is assigned to read *The Orchids and Gumbo Poker Club*, which is about a mother and daughter's relationship. She loves the book and wants to get closer to her own mother. Mrs. McGuire is more than happy to spend more time with Lizzie. They make pottery together and act like best friends. But when Mrs. McGuire tells Lizzie things that are hard for a kid to hear—like her grandmother wants to leave her grandfather and Mr. McGuire was once in trouble with the Internal Revenue Service—Lizzie wishes she could go back to just being "the kid."

Seeing Lizzie spend time with her mom, Miranda and Gordo decide to try hanging with their parents. Gordo asks his dad to go fishing, and Miranda asks her mom to go shopping. But Miranda's shopping spree isn't as fun as she thought, and Gordo is sprayed by a skunk before he even gets to the fishing hole. All three kids decide they like hanging out together more than being their parents' "friends."

Meanwhile, a pesky chimpanzee finds its way to the McGuire house and wreaks havoc, which gets blamed on Matt. Finally, Mr. McGuire sees the chimp, and lets Matt off the hook.

DID YOU KNOW?

Um, Mom? Too much information!

- "Mom's Best Friend" was ranked as the second-highest-rated of all the *Lizzie* telecasts. (Ratings were measured among kids ages 6 to 11 on March 8, 2002.)

- This episode earned *Lizzie McGuire* the Gracie Allen Award, from the American Women in Radio and Television, for its positive portrayal of women.

- *The Orchids and Gumbo Poker Club* was a made-up book, but after this episode aired, Disney Press created and published it—complete with Lizzie's notes, jokes, and doodles in the margin.

- Mr. McGuire's cousin Ree Ree is mentioned and pictured in this episode.

- In this episode, viewers learn that Mr. McGuire's Social Security number is one digit away from Bill Gates's. (which is how he got into trouble with the Internal Revenue Service!)

- The chimp's owners are Jeremy Bargiel and David Alex Rosen, who also appear in episode #21 "Rated Aargh!" and episode #30 "Gordo's Bar Mitzvah."

CAN YOU SPOT THE BLOOPERS?

- Lizzie tells her mom it's an Orchids and Gumbo Poker "Society" when it's actually a "Club."

- Talking about her parents, Mrs. McGuire says "Grandma" Chuck instead of "Grandpa."

- When Lizzie and her mom are making pottery, the amount of clay on Lizzie's nose changes from shot to shot.

77

EPISODE NUMBER 37:
"THE RISE AND FALL
OF THE KATE EMPIRE"

DIRECTOR: Anson Williams
WRITERS: Nina G. Bargiel & Jeremy J. Bargiel
EXECUTIVE PRODUCERS: Stan Rogow & Susan Estelle Jansen
CONSULTING PRODUCERS: Douglas Tuber & Tim Maile
PRODUCER: Jill Danton
SERIES CREATED BY: Terri Minsky
CAST STARS: Hilary Duff (Lizzie McGuire),
Lalaine (Miranda Sanchez),
Adam Lamberg
(David "Gordo" Gordon),
Jake Thomas (Matt McGuire),
Hallie Todd (Jo McGuire), and
Robert Carradine (Sam McGuire)
GUEST STARS: Christian Copelin (Lanny Onasis),
Ashlie Brillault (Kate Sanders),
Davida Williams (Claire Miller)

WHAT HAPPENS?

When Kate dislocates her shoulder at cheerleading practice, she's suddenly a social outcast. Former best friend Claire refuses to let her sit at the cheerleader table and teases her. Kate is forced to sit on the ground and hang out in the dork hallway. Even though Lizzie, Miranda, and Gordo want to be happy that Kate has lost her cheerleader superpowers, they discover that life with Claire as the most popular girl in school isn't fun. She makes everyone sit on the ground at lunch. She's even worse than Kate!

Lizzie, Gordo, and Miranda set out to make Kate popular again, and Lizzie teaches Kate one-armed gymnastics. At cheerleading practice, Kate wows the other cheerleaders with her newly learned skills, and Claire hurts her wrist trying to show up Kate. Lizzie wonders if her good deeds taught Kate anything, and she's happy to see Kate treat Claire with more kindness than Claire treated Kate.

At home, Matt has landed a one-line role in the school play and it goes to his head. He alienates his parents and Lanny. But when Matt loses his voice right before the play, he loses the role to Lanny.

DID YOU KNOW?

- Hilary Duff does her own gymnastics in this episode.

- "Spinnin' Around" by Jump 5 plays when Lizzie teaches Kate gymnastics.

- When Lizzie refers to her rhythmic gymnastics days, she's talking about events that took place in episode #4 "I've Got Rhythmic."

- Miranda and Gordo sing "Ding-Dong! The Witch Is Dead," from the feature film *The Wizard of Oz*.

- This episode's title, "The Rise and Fall of the Kate Empire," is a Lizzie-fication of the famous book title *The Rise and Fall of the Roman Empire* by Edward Gibbon, who also wrote *The Decline and Fall of the Roman Empire*.

> I can't believe I'm helping Kate!

CAN YOU SPOT THE BLOOPERS?

- When Lizzie is talking to Kate in the "dork" hallway, Lizzie's purse is on her shoulder, then gone, then on her shoulder again.

**EPISODE NUMBER 38:
"OVER THE HILL"**

DIRECTOR: Savage Steve Holland
WRITER: Alison Taylor
EXECUTIVE PRODUCERS: Stan Rogow & Susan Estelle Jansen
CONSULTING PRODUCERS: Douglas Tuber & Tim Maile
PRODUCER: Jill Danton
SERIES CREATED BY: Terri Minsky
CAST STARS: Hilary Duff (Lizzie McGuire),
　　Lalaine (Miranda Sanchez),
　　Adam Lamberg
　　　(David "Gordo" Gordon),
　　Jake Thomas (Matt McGuire),
　　Hallie Todd (Jo McGuire), and
　　Robert Carradine (Sam McGuire)
GUEST STARS: Christian Copelin (Lanny Onasis),
　　Ashlie Brillault (Kate Sanders),
　　Clayton Snyder (Ethan Craft),
　　Carly Schroeder (Malina)
COSTARS: Anastasia Baranova (Cara Gunther),
　　Grayce Wey (Assistant),
　　Brad Grunberg (Chauffeur),
　　Jeremy Bargiel (Friend #1),
　　David Alex Rosen (Friend #2)

WHAT HAPPENS?

Lizzie wonders what she'll be in the future, since she doesn't have any special talents or dreams. Miranda knows she wants to be a successful violinist and Gordo plans on becoming a famous director, but what about Lizzie? When Lizzie has a nightmare that she's working at a fast-food drive-through as an old woman, and both Miranda and Gordo have long forgotten her, she really freaks out. She's even more worried when a girl at school makes it to the Olympics. She fantasizes about different future careers, like being the scientist who clones the bald eagle—after it goes extinct. Then she imagines being a stay-at-home mom, but her perfect husband isn't Ethan, it's Gordo! That brings her back down to earth and she realizes that she has plenty of time to figure out who she is.

Meanwhile, after watching a horror movie, Matt is scared in his own house. He's convinced there's a ghost and tries feng shui to get rid of the spirits. Finally, Mr. McGuire asks his softball buddies to pretend to be Ghostbusters, but when they trip on the porch, they discover that a litter of puppies under the floor is the "presence" Matt felt.

What am I going to be when I grow up? Someone please tell me now!

- Costume designer Cathryn Wagner lists this episode as one of her top three favorites. "The futuristic burger drive-through costume was a costume we made at the studio," she said, "and we tried to make her as haggard as possible. Also, I made the race-car-driver jumpsuit. We constructed all the patches on it, and they say things like 'Gordo's Auto Shop' and 'McGuire Lube and Oil,' since we couldn't use real auto shops and logos."

- This is the first time Miranda's goal of being a professional violinist is mentioned. Usually, Miranda's other musical interest is featured—singing.

- Lizzie references the film *The Sixth Sense* when talking about Matt.

- Brad Grunberg, who played the security guard in "Here Comes Aaron Carter," plays Gordo's chauffeur in this episode.

CAN YOU SPOT THE BLOOPERS?

- In the beginning, Lizzie falls headfirst into an empty trash can, but the next shot shows her standing in the trash can covered with trash.

- When Matt and his dad are watching the horror movie, the amount of popcorn in Mr. McGuire's bowl changes from shot to shot.

EPISODE NUMBER 39: "INNER BEAUTY"

DIRECTOR: Mark Rosman
WRITER: Melissa Gould
EXECUTIVE PRODUCERS: Stan Rogow & Susan Estelle Jansen
CONSULTING PRODUCERS: Douglas Tuber & Tim Maile
PRODUCER: Jill Danton
SERIES CREATED BY: Terri Minsky
CAST STARS: Hilary Duff (Lizzie McGuire),
Lalaine (Miranda Sanchez),
Adam Lamberg
(David "Gordo" Gordon),
Jake Thomas (Matt McGuire),
Hallie Todd (Jo McGuire), and
Robert Carradine (Sam McGuire)
GUEST STARS: Christian Copelin (Lanny Onasis),
Travis Payne (Stern Teacher)

WHAT HAPPENS?

When Miranda and Lizzie are rehearsing for a music video that
Gordo is directing, Gordo makes a sarcastic comment about the girls
eating too much. The next day, Miranda, who is already stressed
about her grades, thinks she looks fat in one of the pictures Gordo
has taken. At lunch, she doesn't eat, and that evening at Lizzie's house
she almost passes out while dancing. Lizzie tries to talk to Miranda
about not eating. But Miranda won't listen. Lizzie's mom agrees to talk
to Miranda's mother if Miranda doesn't snap out of it soon.

When Lizzie, Miranda, and Gordo begin to film the video, Lizzie
and Gordo confront Miranda about not eating. At first Miranda is
angry, but Lizzie insists they care about her and she's scaring them.
Miranda admits that she hasn't been eating because she's been so
stressed about school and her future. She promises to start eating
again and the video shoot goes great. Later at Lizzie's house, the trio
watch the video and Miranda can't get over how great she looks.

Meanwhile, Matt's teacher tells his parents that he has artistic
potential, so they encourage Matt. But his creativity gets out of
control when he uses Mr. McGuire's car as a canvas!

DID YOU KNOW?

- Costume designer Cathryn Wagner lists this episode as her all-time favorite because of the music video that Gordo makes. "I love the black and white satin blouses that Lizzie and Miranda wore," she said. "They were mirror images of each other ... and that showed teamwork to me. No one was the 'star' and that showed the friendship of the two girls."

- The song in Gordo's music video is "Us Against the World" by Play. This same song is also used in the episode titled "The Courtship of Miranda Sanchez."

- Gordo's music video is titled "Detention."

- The info notes on the video say it is made by "Rosman Records." Mark Rosman is the director of this episode!

- The year this episode first aired (2002), Disney Channel's *Lizzie McGuire* was awarded the Imagen Award in Best Children's Program, Live Action category, for its positive portrayal of Latino culture.

CAN YOU SPOT THE BLOOPERS?

- When Lanny is holding Matt's artist pad and Matt draws a picture of Lizzie, the already-drawn picture of Lizzie is visible under Lanny's arm.

- When they arrive at the video shoot, Lizzie's hair is up and Miranda's is down, but in the video, Lizzie's hair is down and Miranda's is up.

DIRECTOR: Savage Steve Holland

WRITER: Alison Taylor

EXECUTIVE PRODUCERS: Stan Rogow & Susan Estelle Jansen

CONSULTING PRODUCERS: Douglas Tuber & Tim Maile

PRODUCER: Jill Danton

SERIES CREATED BY: Terri Minsky

CAST STARS: Hilary Duff (Lizzie McGuire),
Lalaine (Miranda Sanchez),
Adam Lamberg
(David "Gordo" Gordon),
Jake Thomas (Matt McGuire),
Hallie Todd (Jo McGuire), and
Robert Carradine (Sam McGuire)

GUEST STARS: Ashlie Brillault (Kate Sanders),
Zachary Quinto (Director),
Audrey Wasilewski (Assistant Robyn)

COSTARS: Haylie Duff (Cousin Amy),
Rachelle Carson (Donna Pinto),
Cory Hodges (Student),
Adam King (Boy Singer #1),
Shad Sager (Boy Singer #2),
Josh Martinez (Boy Singer #3)

EPISODE NUMBER 40: "PARTY OVER HERE"

WHAT HAPPENS?

Kate is having a birthday party, and her mom makes her invite everyone at school, including Lizzie, Miranda, and Gordo. Lizzie and Miranda aren't allowed to go because the only chaperone will be Kate's eighteen-year-old cousin Amy. Gordo is allowed to go, so Miranda and Lizzie lie and say they're going to the mall, but then sneak over to Kate's party.

When they get there, they find the party swarming with Cousin Amy's older friends. The rowdy partygoers knock Kate into her own birthday cake, and she is humiliated. Then the older kids really start wrecking her house and Lizzie knows this is a job for her mom, so she calls her. Mrs. McGuire comes over, chases everyone out of the house, and helps the kids clean up. Kate is grateful, and Lizzie gets grounded. Meanwhile, the McGuire men have been chosen to star in a commercial for a new sports drink, Cardio Punch.

DID YOU KNOW?

● Hilary Duff's sister, Haylie, plays Cousin Amy in this episode (as well as episodes #63 Clue-Less and #64 Xtreme Xmas).

Wow, Kate's life isn't perfect either . . . who knew?

● Actress, songwriter, singer Haylie Duff is two years older than Hilary. (Haylie's birthday is February 19, 1985, and Hilary's is September 28, 1987.)

● Haylie wrote the song "Girl in the Band" for *The Lizzie McGuire Movie* sound track and sang it with Hilary.

● Kate claims this birthday party is for her "fourteenth birthday," but in "Gordo's Video," viewers learned that she was already fourteen because she was held back in kindergarten. So you'll notice that when Mrs. McGuire mentions that she's turning fifteen, Kate corrects her, saying she's fourteen. Mrs. McGuire says "right," and Lizzie, Gordo, and Miranda snicker—because, like the viewers, they know Kate is really fifteen!

CAN YOU SPOT THE BLOOPERS?

● When Lizzie and Miranda leave the mall bathroom after getting ready for the party, their outfits are different from the ones they wear at the bus stop and at Kate's house.

DIRECTOR: Anson Williams
WRITERS: Nina G. Bargiel & Jeremy J. Bargiel
EXECUTIVE PRODUCERS: Stan Rogow & Susan Estelle Jansen
CO-EXECUTIVE PRODUCERS: Douglas Tuber & Tim Maile
PRODUCER: Jill Danton
SERIES CREATED BY: Terri Minsky
CAST STARS: Hilary Duff (Lizzie McGuire),
Lalaine (Miranda Sanchez),
Adam Lamberg
(David "Gordo" Gordon),
Jake Thomas (Matt McGuire),
Hallie Todd (Jo McGuire), and
Robert Carradine (Sam McGuire)
GUEST STARS: Ashlie Brillault (Kate Sanders),
Carly Schroeder (Melina Bianco),
Davida Williams (Claire Miller),
Keili Lefkovitz (Manager)
COSTARS: Nicholas E. Barb (Reggie),
Brian Kimmet (Spoon Guy),
Tom Mastrantonio (Muffin Man)

WHAT HAPPENS?

Lizzie wants a raise in her allowance, but her parents say no way, so she gets a job as a busboy at the Digital Bean. Her parents are worried at first that Lizzie won't have time for her studies, but she assures them she'll be fine. Lizzie is excited at the thought of earning her own money, but she soon finds out work is harder than she thought it would be. Her manager is strict and won't let Lizzie take a break or talk to anyone.

When Matt comes to ask Lizzie for advice about Melina, who's paying attention to another boy, Lizzie doesn't have time for him. Miranda offers him advice, and Matt soon has a crush on *her*. While Lizzie is working her tail off, Miranda is busy trying to ditch Matt. Lizzie starts to wish she was unemployed, and the last straw is when three customers (including Claire) drive her crazy all at once, and she tells them all off. Lizzie is fired, but she's secretly glad.

Meanwhile, Melina has heard that Matt likes Miranda and goes to the McGuire house to get her man back. Miranda is happy to get rid of him!

DID YOU KNOW?

- Lizzie is fourteen in this episode, even though there has been no episode marking her birthday.

Whoa. Who knew work would be so much . . . work!

- This episode's title is taken from the film *Working Girl*, starring Melanie Griffith and Harrison Ford.

- Despite the fact that *Lizzie McGuire* is centered on a junior high school girl's trials and tribulations, not all of the show's fans are kids— or even their parents. "*Lizzie McGuire* started out having a younger audience," said actress Hilary Duff in an MTV interview, "but then as the show kept going on, older and older people would come up to me telling me how much they love my show—like college students!"

CAN YOU SPOT THE BLOOPERS?

- Matt hands Miranda a card, which changes from green to yellow from different angles.

- When Lizzie slips on the smoothie, she's on her stomach, but in the next shot, she's on her back.

87

EPISODE NUMBER 42:
"AND THE WINNER IS"

DIRECTOR: Peter Montgomery
WRITER: Melissa Gould
EXECUTIVE PRODUCERS: Stan Rogow & Susan Estelle Jansen
CO-EXECUTIVE PRODUCERS: Douglas Tuber & Tim Maile
SUPERVISING PRODUCER: Melissa Gould
PRODUCER: Jill Danton
SERIES CREATED BY: Terri Minsky
CAST STARS: Hilary Duff (Lizzie McGuire),
Lalaine (Miranda Sanchez),
Adam Lamberg
(David "Gordo" Gordon),
Jake Thomas (Matt McGuire),
Hallie Todd (Jo McGuire), and
Robert Carradine (Sam McGuire)
GUEST STARS: Ashlie Brillault (Kate Sanders),
Clayton Snyder (Ethan Craft),
Kyle J. Downes (Larry Tudgeman),
Arvie Lowe, Jr. (Mr. Dig)

WHAT HAPPENS?

Lizzie, Miranda, and Gordo are furious with each other over a misunderstanding when they are assigned to go on a scavenger hunt in Mr. Dig's class. Because they're not speaking, Lizzie pairs with Ethan Craft, Miranda partners with Larry Tudgeman, and Gordo with Kate Sanders.

As the three teams trek through the city, looking for Mr. Dig's clues, Lizzie, Miranda, and Gordo tell their partners why they're angry. It's all a big mix-up about meeting up at the Digital Bean.

Lizzie doesn't know that her little brother Matt is also following the clues. He finds Lizzie's assignment sheet and thinks there's a real treasure to be found. When he crosses the finish line before anyone else, he's disappointed to find no treasure, except for some pocket change and a bus token.

Ethan, Larry, and Kate all tell their partners that they're lucky to have the type of friends that they do. Lizzie, Miranda, and Gordo can't believe that Ethan, Larry, and Kate are right, and they start to reconsider how they feel. Just as Ethan and Lizzie are about to cross the finish line, she sees Miranda, Larry, Gordo, and Kate close behind. She stops to make up with her friends, then all three teams cross the finish line together.

DID YOU KNOW?

Why do I have to apologize if I know I'm right?

- In this episode, Larry Tudgeman's hair has blond highlights.

- In the music store, the CD holding the clue is *Key of a Minor*, by recording artist Jessica Riddle.

- When they're doing the race, "Perfect Day" by Hoku plays. The song is also featured on the sound track for the movie *Legally Blonde*.

- Kate calls Lizzie "Blade Runner," referring to the science-fiction movie of the same name, starring Harrison Ford.

CAN YOU SPOT THE BLOOPERS?

- When Mr. McGuire sprays whipped cream in his mouth, some gets on his shirt, but it is missing in another shot.

- In one scene, Gordo accidentally elbows Lizzie in the face.

EPISODE NUMBER 43:
"IN MIRANDA LIZZIE
DOES NOT TRUST"

DIRECTOR: Alan Cohn
WRITERS: Douglas Tuber & Tim Maile
EXECUTIVE PRODUCERS: Stan Rogow & Susan Estelle Jansen
CO-EXECUTIVE PRODUCERS: Douglas Tuber & Tim Maile
SUPERVISING PRODUCER: Melissa Gould
PRODUCER: Jill Danton
SERIES CREATED BY: Terri Minsky
CAST STARS: Hilary Duff (Lizzie McGuire),
Lalaine (Miranda Sanchez),
Adam Lamberg
(David "Gordo" Gordon),
Jake Thomas (Matt McGuire),
Hallie Todd (Jo McGuire), and
Robert Carradine (Sam McGuire)
GUEST STARS: Christian Copelin (Lanny Onasis),
Arvie Lowe, Jr. (Mr. Dig),
Candy Brown Houston (Mrs. Stebel),
Greg Baker (Security Guard)
COSTARS: Clayton Snyder (Ethan Craft),
Cassie Walker (Beth),
Evan Lee Dahl (Jackson)

WHAT HAPPENS?

At the mall, Lizzie and Gordo are shocked
when Miranda dumps a ton of free candy in her purse.
While shopping, she bumps into a lipstick display and hurriedly
puts the fallen lipsticks back. The store security guard, who'd been
watching, stops Miranda and checks her purse. He finds a lipstick from
the store and accuses her of stealing it. Miranda swears she bought it the
week before, but Lizzie can't back her up because she wasn't there. Miranda
is taken to the back office, but later calls Lizzie to tell her she is upset that
Lizzie doesn't trust her. In gym class, the girls must partner for a dance, but
they end up in a huge fight instead.

At the McGuire house, Matt and Lanny start their own Internet talk show.
Their ratings are low until Mr. McGuire stumbles onto the set and his
clumsiness makes their ratings soar. The show becomes a comedy of
pranks and pratfalls, and Lanny storms off the set, unhappy with the
new direction. Later, he calls Matt with a problem and Matt
rushes to help him. Lizzie is surprised that even Matt
knows the value of a true friendship, and she
apologizes to Miranda for not
believing her.

DID YOU KNOW?

- In this episode, we learn that Mr. and Mrs. McGuire have been married for fifteen years.

- We also find out that Lanny's last name is Onasis.

- Lanny's father owns peacocks.

- The actor who plays Mr. Dig, Arvie Lowe, Jr., does all his own dance steps in this episode because he is a professional dancer in real life. In fact, Lowe's professional career began at age twelve when he went on the road as a dancer for Reebok footwear. He performed in New York City, Chicago, Atlanta, Paris, and Germany. He has appeared in several videos and television shows, including *Sister, Sister* and *Moesha*, as well as feature films, including *Newsies*.

Oh, I just don't know what to believe!

CAN YOU SPOT THE BLOOPERS?

- Mr. Dig mispronounces Beth Ludberg's name by calling her Beth Lubderg.

- Before Miranda nearly empties the candy bowl, it's full. Then after she puts the candy in her purse, it's full again!

EPISODE NUMBER 44:
"THE LONGEST YARD"

DIRECTOR: Steve De Jarnatt
WRITERS: Jeremy J. Bargiel & Nina G. Bargiel
EXECUTIVE PRODUCERS: Stan Rogow & Susan Estelle Jansen
COEXECUTIVE PRODUCERS: Douglas Tuber & Tim Maile
SUPERVISING PRODUCER: Melissa Gould
PRODUCER: Jill Danton
SERIES CREATED BY: Terri Minsky
CAST STARS: Hilary Duff (Lizzie McGuire),
Lalaine (Miranda Sanchez),
Adam Lamberg
(David "Gordo" Gordon),
Jake Thomas (Matt McGuire),
Hallie Todd (Jo McGuire), and
Robert Carradine (Sam McGuire)
GUEST STARS: Christian Copelin (Lanny Onasis),
Jeremy Bargiel (Jeremy),
David Alex Rosen (David)

WHAT HAPPENS?

When Mrs. McGuire is roped into going to the Super Sports Expo with Mr. McGuire, Lizzie must babysit Matt and Lanny. She catches them taking her father's prized possession, a Walter Payton—signed football, to play a game in the backyard. Lizzie reclaims the ball and hides it in the closet. But when Matt and Lanny try to get a board game from the closet shelf, they knock a bowling ball onto Mr. McGuire's football, ruining it. Matt and Lanny travel all around town trying to get the ball fixed.

When Lizzie discovers that the boys are missing, she and Miranda go looking for them. They end up at a collector's store and find Matt and Lanny trying to convince the clerk to let them trade it for another Walter Payton ball. He refuses, but Lizzie talks him into trading their Walter Payton ball for a Dick Butkus ball. In the end, Matt and Lizzie both realize how much they care about each other when they see how worried Lizzie was about Matt. Later, the kids are shocked to find out that Mrs. McGuire had already ruined the original Walter Payton ball and replaced it with a fake!

DID YOU KNOW?

- In this episode, Lizzie makes a reference to the movie *The Time Machine*.

What is it with guys and football anyway?

- Walter Payton and Dick Butkus, the sports figures whose autographs are prized, were both Chicago Bears.

- Mr. McGuire's friends who check on the kids were portrayed as big Bears fans in episode #30 "Gordo's Bar Mitzvah."

CAN YOU SPOT THE BLOOPERS?

- When Sam talks to his football, there's a brown vase beside it. When Matt takes the ball, the vase is gone.

- There are red pillows on the couch when Gordo is watching TV, but these pillows are gone later when Mr. McGuire's buddies are sitting on the couch.

EPISODE NUMBER 45: "THOSE FREAKY MCGUIRES"

DIRECTOR: Oz Scott
WRITER: Melissa Gould
EXECUTIVE PRODUCERS: Stan Rogow & Susan Estelle Jansen
COEXECUTIVE PRODUCERS: Douglas Tuber & Tim Maile
SUPERVISING PRODUCER: Melissa Gould
PRODUCER: Jill Danton
SERIES CREATED BY: Terri Minsky
CAST STARS: Hilary Duff (Lizzie McGuire),
Lalaine (Miranda Sanchez),
Adam Lamberg
(David "Gordo" Gordon),
Jake Thomas (Matt McGuire),
Hallie Todd (Jo McGuire), and
Robert Carradine (Sam McGuire)
GUEST STARS: Christian Copelin (Lanny Onasis),
Ashlie Brillault (Kate Sanders),
Clayton Snyder (Ethan Craft),
Kyle J. Downes (Larry Tudgeman),
Carly Schroeder (Melina Bianco)
COSTAR: Matteo Crismani (Clark)

WHAT HAPPENS?

After a huge fight, Lizzie and Matt scream "I'll stay out of your life!" but as they say that, something happens and they switch bodies. They try to switch back but it doesn't work, and their parents won't let them stay home from school. So, Matt (who's actually Lizzie) heads off to school dressed as a nerd, and Lizzie (who's really Matt) goes to school in a horribly mismatched outfit.

Miranda and Gordo are totally confused, but they have to admit they've never seen Lizzie so confident. She and Ethan Craft share stories and she even tells off Kate. When Kate pulls a prank to make Lizzie look bad, Lizzie (with Matt's creativity) pulls an even bigger one on Kate. Meanwhile, Matt (really Lizzie) can't understand why he gets blamed at school for things he didn't even do. Melina and Lanny help him pay back the real prankster.

That evening, Matt and Lizzie realize they helped each other solve some problems, but they wish they had their own bodies. In the middle of the night, they return to normal. Was it real? Or just a dream?

Puh-leeeeeease tell me I'm dreaming!

* This episode contains the "Most Embarassing Moment," as selected by the viewers during a Disney Channel broadcast of "A Raven New Year's Eve," December 31, 2002. This was the moment: Matt (in Lizzie's body) rigs up a very messy trap for Kate Sanders. As she opens her locker, science-lab frogs jump out at her. She screams, terrified and disgusted, and goes running down the hall, where she slips on a pile of banana peels and goes careening into a doorway, where a rigged bucket of chili comes pouring down on top of her. And, of course, half the school witnesses it.

* This episode's story was a takeoff of the Disney movie *Freaky Friday*, in which a teenage daughter and her mother switch bodies.

* When Lizzie is in Matt's body, she can actually understand what Lanny, who never speaks, is saying!

CAN YOU SPOT THE BLOOPERS?

* Matt and Lizzie try to switch back by repeating what they yelled. However, when they try to switch back, they say "Stay out of my life!" but what they are supposed to say is, "I'll stay out of your life!" (Maybe that's why it didn't work!)

* When Kate slips on the bananas and slides down the hall, she's on her stomach, but as the chili falls on her head, she's on her back.

* At the end, Mr. McGuire walks out of his room without his glasses, then before he heads back into his room he's wearing his glasses.

EPISODE NUMBER 46:
"A GORDO STORY"

DIRECTOR:	Savage Steve Holland
WRITERS:	Jeremy J. Bargiel & Nina G. Bargiel
EXECUTIVE PRODUCERS:	Stan Rogow & Susan Estelle Jansen
COEXECUTIVE PRODUCERS:	Douglas Tuber & Tim Maile
SUPERVISING PRODUCER:	Melissa Gould
PRODUCER:	Jill Danton
SERIES CREATED BY:	Terri Minsky
CAST STARS:	Hilary Duff (Lizzie McGuire), Lalaine (Miranda Sanchez), Adam Lamberg (David "Gordo" Gordon), Jake Thomas (Matt McGuire), Hallie Todd (Jo McGuire), and Robert Carradine (Sam McGuire)
GUEST STARS:	Christian Copelin (Lanny Onasis), Clayton Snyder (Ethan Craft), Arvie Lowe, Jr. (Mr. Dig), Chelsea J. Wilson (Parker McKenzie)
COSTARS:	Tricia Cruz (Mrs. Varga), Brendan Hill (Student)

WHAT HAPPENS?

At the Digital Bean, Gordo asks Parker McKenzie to the upcoming school dance, but she says "I can't." Lizzie asks Parker why, and she says it's because Gordo is short. Gordo overhears this and is hurt. The next day at school, he walks in wearing high-heeled cowboy boots and acts obsessed with his height. He claims he's okay with Parker turning him down, but when Miranda says Parker is going to the dance with Ethan, he becomes upset.

Gordo goes to Mr. Dig for advice, who tells him that who he is inside is what counts. Gordo has a heart-to-heart with Lizzie and all three friends go to the dance together.

At the dance, they see Parker having a terrible time with Ethan, who's an extremely embarrassing dancer. Parker asks Gordo to dance and he forgives her. After Miranda finds a dance partner, Lizzie says she's cool to hang by herself, but she's a little sad. Could she possibly have feelings for Gordo?

Meanwhile, Matt is bored by his own family history and makes up a far-fetched fake one for a class project.

DID YOU KNOW?

Even guys get insecure? Who knew?

- When Gordo is obsessing over his height, the song "I Wish" by Skee-lo plays. Lyrics talk about wanting to be taller.

- Gordo tries to tell Parker the King of Norway joke he told in episode #44 "The Longest Yard."

- The original title of this episode was "Inner Beauty II: A Gordo Story" because it is the Part Two version of episode #39 "Inner Beauty," in which Miranda also obsesses about her appearance.

- In this episode, we learn Lanny is related to historic figure Crispus Attucks, the first American to be killed in the Revolutionary War.

- Kate does not appear in this episode, even though it involves a dance and Kate usually heads every dance committee!

CAN YOU SPOT THE BLOOPERS?

- At the beginning of the episode, Mr. McGuire is peeling a potato. In one shot, it's almost completely peeled, and in the next shot, there is much more skin on the potato.

- When Mr. Dig holds a basketball while talking to Gordo, the placement of the ball changes from shot to shot.

97

DIRECTOR: Peter Montgomery
WRITER: Alison Taylor
EXECUTIVE PRODUCERS: Stan Rogow & Susan Estelle Jansen
COEXECUTIVE PRODUCERS: Douglas Tuber & Tim Maile
SUPERVISING PRODUCER: Melissa Gould
PRODUCER: Jill Danton
SERIES CREATED BY: Terri Minsky
CAST STARS: Hilary Duff (Lizzie McGuire),
Lalaine (Miranda Sanchez),
Adam Lamberg
(David "Gordo" Gordon),
Jake Thomas (Matt McGuire),
Hallie Todd (Jo McGuire), and
Robert Carradine (Sam McGuire)
GUEST STARS: Christian Copelin (Lanny Onasis),
Ashlie Brillault (Kate Sanders),
Clayton Snyder (Ethan Craft),
Kyle J. Downes (Larry Tudgeman)
SPECIAL GUEST STAR: Phill Lewis (Principal Tweedy)

WHAT HAPPENS?

The Spring Fling dance is around the corner and Lizzie is paired with Kate on the decoration committee. When Kate and Lizzie are scoping out the schoolyard for outdoor dancing, Kate knocks over the statue of the school's first principal, breaking its head off. Kate couldn't care less about it, but Lizzie is really worried. She hides the statue's head in her book bag until she can figure out what to do.

Meanwhile, Miranda is excited because Cody Pierson asked her to the dance, and she can't wait to go. Soon, word gets around school that the statue is broken and Principal Tweedy tells the kids that until someone confesses, there will be no school dance. For Miranda's sake, Lizzie takes the blame for the statue the next day at school. The dance is back on, but she's not allowed to go. When everyone is at the dance, a disappointed Lizzie sits at home. Matt is also sad. Ever since he and Lanny raised money to buy a bike to share, they never spend time together anymore.

Lizzie is suddenly cheered up, however, when everyone at school brings the dance to her house. While Kate is at school, all alone at the dance, there's a major party going on at Lizzie's!

DID YOU KNOW?

Sometimes being nice stinks!

 In this episode, Lizzie carries a pink backpack instead of her usual blue backpack. This is obviously because the pink backpack is bigger than her blue one and can fit the statue's head!

 Lizzie's bedroom phone is red again, as it was in the episode "First Kiss." Lizzie's phone is usually purple.

🌸 The title of this episode was inspired by the famous play *You're a Good Man, Charlie Brown*.

CAN YOU SPOT THE BLOOPERS?

🌸 When Gordo is talking to Lizzie about an escape plan, her left pigtail moves from in front of her shoulder to behind her shoulder.

🌸 When Lizzie is crying and talking to her mother, the shots from behind clearly show her saying something other than what is heard.

DIRECTOR: Tim O'Donnell

WRITER: Bob Thomas

EXECUTIVE PRODUCERS: Stan Rogow & Susan Estelle Jansen

COEXECUTIVE PRODUCERS: Douglas Tuber & Tim Maile

SUPERVISING PRODUCER: Melissa Gould

PRODUCER: Jill Danton

SERIES CREATED BY: Terri Minsky

CAST STARS: Hilary Duff (Lizzie McGuire),
Lalaine (Miranda Sanchez),
Adam Lamberg
(David "Gordo" Gordon),
Jake Thomas (Matt McGuire),
Hallie Todd (Jo McGuire), and
Robert Carradine (Sam McGuire)

GUEST STAR: Kyle J. Downes (Larry Tudgeman)

EPISODE NUMBER 48: "BEST DRESSED FOR MUCH LESS"

WHAT HAPPENS?

Voting for the "Class Best" list is coming up and Lizzie is fed up with the popular kids taking all the glory. Lizzie decides she'll try to win Best Dressed, but she'll need some cool new clothes to beat Kate. She finds the perfect pair of jeans, but they cost $65. Mrs. McGuire says no way! Instead, she offers to help Lizzie bargain shop for a new outfit. Lizzie shudders at the word *bargain*, so she secretly pools money with Miranda and Gordo to buy the expensive jeans. Mrs. McGuire goes shopping for Lizzie anyway, and comes home with some great buys.

At school, Lizzie changes into the expensive jeans she secretly bought, only to have them ruined. She's forced to change back into the bargain jeans that her mom bought. To Lizzie's surprise, everyone asks where she got them. She can't tell them because she didn't go shopping with her mom, and she wishes she had.

Meanwhile, Matt appears on a local kids show and is suddenly famous with the young crowd. The fame quickly goes to Matt's head, but he's brought back down to earth when the show is canceled.

DID YOU KNOW?

Bargain shopping? Don't even go there.

- Bob Thomas, who wrote this episode, is the father of Jake Thomas, who plays Matt.

- It's Claire who actually ends up winning the Best Dressed title in this episode.

- Sam is shown reading *Modern Gnome* magazine.

- An alternate title for this episode was "Kiss My Budget."

- When Matt is being chased around the mall because of his sudden fame, the song "Fame" by singer David Bowie can be heard.

- Brief film clips from other episodes appear in this one. Can you identify them? Here are two hints. In one episode, Lizzie gets a job at Digital Bean. In another, Lizzie freaks over a copycat.

CAN YOU SPOT THE BLOOPERS?

- When the kids pull Matt's right sleeve off, his left sleeve is gone, too. Then, in the next shot, his left sleeve is back on.

- Sam takes a picture for a young fan of Matt's, but after the photo is snapped, Sam never appears to give the camera back to the fan.

- The slushy spills on both Lizzie and Gordo, but after Lizzie changes, Gordo has no slushy on him.

EPISODE NUMBER 49:
"JUST FRIENDS"

DIRECTOR:	Mark Rosman
WRITERS:	Douglas Tuber & Tim Maile
EXECUTIVE PRODUCERS:	Stan Rogow & Susan Estelle Jansen
COEXECUTIVE PRODUCERS:	Douglas Tuber & Tim Maile
SUPERVISING PRODUCER:	Melissa Gould
PRODUCER:	Jill Danton
SERIES CREATED BY:	Terri Minsky
CAST STARS:	Hilary Duff (Lizzie McGuire), Lalaine (Miranda Sanchez), Adam Lamberg (David "Gordo" Gordon), Jake Thomas (Matt McGuire), Hallie Todd (Jo McGuire), and Robert Carradine (Sam McGuire)
GUEST STARS:	Christian Copelin (Lanny Onasis), Clayton Snyder (Ethan Craft), Kyle J. Downes (Larry Tudgeman)
COSTARS:	Jake Blakey (Sonny), Jacob Price (Drinking Kid), Maurice Maslen (Pope look-a-like)

WHAT HAPPENS?

Gordo and Miranda convince Lizzie to finally ask her crush-boy Ethan out, so she nervously invites him to an upcoming school dance. But Lizzie is devastated when Ethan turns her down, telling her that he thinks of her as a friend but not as a girlfriend. Lizzie refuses to give up. With the help of Gordo and Miranda, she sets out to find out exactly what type of girl Ethan likes—and then she'll become it. When Ethan says he likes "mysterious" girls, Lizzie sets out to be totally mysterious. She dresses in a long black dress and sunglasses, and she tells Ethan she likes all of the things that he likes—including golf and grape soda.

After she's sure she's reeled him in, Lizzie asks him to the dance a second time, but he still says no! Lizzie is disappointed, but she finally realizes that she shouldn't change herself just to get a guy to like her. She goes home to have a drink at Club Flamingo, the new smoothie-only nightclub Matt has opened in the backyard. Gordo and Miranda join her and they dance their troubles away to the music of Lanny's keyboard.

DID YOU KNOW?

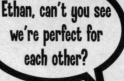

Ethan, can't you see we're perfect for each other?

- Larry Tudgeman is allergic to guacamole.

- In this episode, Gordo wants to be a Bill Gates-type computer tycoon, not a movie director.

- When Larry walks into Club Flamingo and everyone shouts "Tudge!" it's a tribute to the NBC sitcom *Cheers* and the character Norm, played by George Wendt. When Norm entered the bar in *Cheers*, everyone in the bar always shouted, "Norm!"

- Lanny is in the 4-H Club and raises sheep.

CAN YOU SPOT THE BLOOPERS?

- In the beginning scene, from afar, Lizzie pulls up her dress strap. In the next shot, a close-up, she repeats the action.

- When Larry is talking to Matt, the same girl in a yellow-striped shirt walks by twice in the same direction.

DIRECTOR:	Steve De Jarnatt
WRITERS:	Douglas Tuber & Tim Maile
EXECUTIVE PRODUCERS:	Stan Rogow & Susan Estelle Jansen
COEXECUTIVE PRODUCERS:	Douglas Tuber & Tim Maile
SUPERVISING PRODUCER:	Melissa Gould
PRODUCER:	Jill Danton
SERIES CREATED BY:	Terri Minsky
CAST STARS:	Hilary Duff (Lizzie McGuire), Lalaine (Miranda Sanchez), Adam Lamberg (David "Gordo" Gordon), Jake Thomas (Matt McGuire), Hallie Todd (Jo McGuire), and Robert Carradine (Sam McGuire)
GUEST STAR:	Joseph Whipp (Grubby)
COSTARS:	Haley Hudson (Clementine), Josh Wise (Cory), Jack Barrett Phelan (Blacksmith)

WHAT HAPPENS?

While her parents and Matt are excited about the annual
family trip to Grubby Gulch, a tacky Old West town, Lizzie is
dreading the vacation. Luckily, she persuades Gordo and Miranda
to come along for the trip. Unfortunately, Mr. McGuire makes
them get up at 5:30 A.M. to hit the road.

Once they get to Grubby Gulch, Lizzie and her buds find the
place too tacky to endure. They decide to ditch the family and hit
the local mall. Before they go, they visit the Grubby Gulch
refreshment stand, and a cute employee named Cory starts
flirting with Lizzie. Cory's sister, Clementine, likes Gordo, so the
kids plan a triple date—including Cory and Clementine's brother
for Miranda.

At lunch, Mr. McGuire says he bought everyone tickets for the
Old Tyme Revue at 7 P.M., the same time as Lizzie's triple date.
The kids act sick to avoid the Revue, but after Lizzie hears her
parents reminiscing about their family vacations, she feels guilty
and ends up bailing on the date to watch the Revue with her
parents. She's surprised to have a good time after all.

DID YOU KNOW?

Not another cheesy family vacation!

● Haley Hudson, who plays Clementine, also appeared in the 2003 Disney film *Freaky Friday*.

● When the gang is at Grubby Gulch, "Rock This Country" by Shania Twain is played.

● Mentioned but never seen—Heath, the hunky brother of Clementine and Cory, who was supposed to be Miranda's date.

● Miranda and Gordo aren't shown at the Revue, but in snapshots shown at the end, they're pictured there.

CAN YOU SPOT THE BLOOPERS?

● When Lizzie is trying to find out how to pay Gordo and Miranda back for coming on the trip, Mrs. McGuire is walking by, but when they cut to the next shot, she's already standing at the car.

● In the lunch line, Gordo doesn't put "Prospector's Stew" on his plate, but at the table, it's on his plate.

● In the lunch line, Miranda drops her fork but doesn't notice it.

EPISODE NUMBER 51:
"BUNKIES"

DIRECTOR: Anson Williams
WRITER: Bob Thomas
EXECUTIVE PRODUCERS: Stan Rogow & Susan Estelle Jansen
COEXECUTIVE PRODUCERS: Douglas Tuber & Tim Maile
SUPERVISING PRODUCER: Melissa Gould
PRODUCER: Jill Danton
SERIES CREATED BY: Terri Minsky
CAST STARS: Hilary Duff (Lizzie McGuire),
Lalaine (Miranda Sanchez),
Adam Lamberg
(David "Gordo" Gordon),
Jake Thomas (Matt McGuire),
Hallie Todd (Jo McGuire), and
Robert Carradine (Sam McGuire)
GUEST STARS: Clayton Snyder (Ethan Craft),
Ashlie Brillault (Kate Sanders),
Kyle J. Downes (Larry Tudgeman),
Simms Thomas (Ms. Dew),
Lamont Thompson (Construction Guy)
COSTARS: Deance Wyatt (Drama King),
Kimberly Aaberg (Drama Queen),
Nick Huff (Basketball Player)

WHAT HAPPENS?

When a pipe bursts and Matt's room is
flooded, he has to move in with Lizzie until it's fixed.
Both kids are furious about the situation, especially the first
night, when they can't agree on how cool or bright the room
should be. Things aren't any better at school, when Lizzie, Miranda,
and Gordo don't have a place on the "Mural of Togetherness" wall to
put their handprints, because they don't belong to any school cliques.
After Matt and Lizzie keep their father up all night with their arguing, he
removes all of their things from Lizzie's room so they don't have anything
to fight over. Matt and Lizzie see through their dad's plan and start
acting like they adore each other.

Finally, the pipe is fixed (after a shady plumber charges way too
much money) and Matt goes back to his room, leaving Lizzie
to sleep in peace. At school, Lizzie, Gordo, and Miranda
decide that they're their own group, and they
proudly place their handprints at the
top of the wall.

DID YOU KNOW?

- Lizzie shared a room with Matt when she was five years old.

- Matt's favorite singer is "Weird Al" Yankovic, the parody songwriter of such hits as "My Bologna," "Polka Your Eyes Out," "Smells Like Nirvana," "I Think I'm a Clone Now," and "Eat It."

- The year this episode first aired (2003), Hilary Duff was honored with a nomination as Favorite Television Actress for Nickelodeon's 16th Annual Kids' Choice Awards. At the ceremony, she accepted the award for the *Lizzie McGuire* show, which was voted Favorite Television Series. (It also won this award in 2002!)

> Move in with my brother? Hello! Is the garage available?

CAN YOU SPOT THE BLOOPERS?

- At night, when Matt and Lizzie are fighting over the window blinds, it's obviously daylight outside.

- When Lizzie and Matt are turning the fan and light on and off, both items are sitting in the same exact place but changed for the proper scene.

EPISODE NUMBER 52:
"LIZZIE'S AND
MIRANDA'S
MAGIC TRAIN"

DIRECTOR: Henry Cahn
WRITERS: Amy Engelberg & Wendy Engelberg
EXECUTIVE PRODUCERS: Stan Rogow & Susan Estelle Jansen
COEXECUTIVE PRODUCERS: Douglas Tuber & Tim Maile
SUPERVISING PRODUCER: Melissa Gould
PRODUCER: Jill Danton
SERIES CREATED BY: Terri Minsky
CAST STARS: Hilary Duff (Lizzie McGuire),
Lalaine (Miranda Sanchez),
Adam Lamberg
(David "Gordo" Gordon),
Jake Thomas (Matt McGuire),
Hallie Todd (Jo McGuire), and
Robert Carradine (Sam McGuire)
GUEST STARS: Ashlie Brillault (Kate Sanders),
Clayton Snyder (Ethan Craft)
COSTARS: Lyle Kanouse (Daisy),
Sandy Fox (Clover),
Prince Davidson (Kid),
Michael Krepack (Toddler #1),
Ronit Mann (Tour Kid #1)

WHAT HAPPENS?

Lizzie and Miranda admit to each other that they still love a children's show called *Clover and Daisy's Magic Train*. When the live show comes to town, Lizzie and Miranda just have to go, but they're embarrassed. They try to get Matt and Lanny to come along, but they say they're way too old for kids' stuff. Besides, Matt is busy with his newest creation: the dirt museum.

Lizzie, Miranda, and Gordo all go to the kids' show, sing along, and have a great time. But their happiness comes to an end when Kate, who's there with the kids she babysits, sees them and tells the whole school. She calls them babies and makes fun of them, and Lizzie is embarrassed. In the end, Lizzie won't stand for the shame anymore. At lunch, she gives a speech to her class about how everyone should listen to Clover and Daisy's message, then she and Gordo lead a sing-along of a Clover and Daisy song. Everyone actually starts singing, and Kate fumes.

At home, Mrs. McGuire finds out about Matt's "dirt museum" and promptly closes it by cleaning the house!

DID YOU KNOW?

C'mon, admit it: being a little kid can be totally fun!

- In this episode, we learn Gordo likes the band Foo Fighters.

- Lizzie still has a rug in her room with a stain on it from when she accidentally threw up as a little girl.

- Ethan Craft is one of the many older kids who lines up for a tour of Matt's gross dirt museum, which carries the full name of "The McGuire Museum of Dirt, Stains, and Grime."

- In *Clover and Daisy's Magic Train*, Clover is a mouse and Daisy is an elephant.

CAN YOU SPOT THE BLOOPERS?

- When the girls see Ethan at Lizzie's house, they throw the pink ribbons from Lizzie's hair on the ground, and, without picking them up, leave for the show. At the show, however, the ribbons are in Lizzie's hair.

EPISODE NUMBER 53:
"SHE SAID, HE SAID, SHE SAID"

DIRECTOR:	Brian K. Roberts
WRITER:	Melissa Gould
EXECUTIVE PRODUCERS:	Stan Rogow & Susan Estelle Jansen
COEXECUTIVE PRODUCERS:	Douglas Tuber & Tim Maile
SUPERVISING PRODUCER:	Melissa Gould
PRODUCER:	Jill Danton
SERIES CREATED BY:	Terri Minsky
CAST STARS:	Hilary Duff (Lizzie McGuire), Lalaine (Miranda Sanchez), Adam Lamberg (David "Gordo" Gordon), Jake Thomas (Matt McGuire), Hallie Todd (Jo McGuire), and Robert Carradine (Sam McGuire)
GUEST STARS:	Ashlie Brillault (Kate Sanders), Kyle J. Downes (Larry Tudgeman), Christian Copelin (Lanny Onasis), Phill Lewis (Principal Tweedy)

WHAT HAPPENS?

It's the biggest food fight ever at school, and Lizzie, Kate, and Larry Tudgeman all get punished by Principal Tweedy. He tells them to clean the lunchroom and write down who started the fight. As they clean, however, they all have different accounts of how the fight started.

In Kate's version, everyone was so distracted by her beauty that the food fight started by accident. In Larry's fantasy, he's a math genius who has *Matrix*-like powers and the fight started after someone slipped on a banana peel. In Lizzie's version, the truest one, the fight started after she accidentally spilled juice and went to get a napkin. Lizzie realizes that in all three versions, the same kid, Gustav, started the fight every time. Lizzie doesn't want to blame him, because she knows he didn't start it on purpose. After the lunchroom is cleaned, the kids leave a note for Principal Tweedy telling him that although they didn't start the fight, they're not going to blame anyone either.

Meanwhile, Matt and Lanny accidentally get left behind during a class field trip downtown, and they make the most of it!

DID YOU KNOW?

- The letter Lizzie reads aloud at the end is inspired by the 1984 movie *The Breakfast Club*. This is the reason that the movie's theme song, "Don't You Forget About Me" by Simple Minds, is played during the final scene.

- Costume designer, Cathryn Wagner, remembers this episode well. "I had to dress thirty extras and our regular cast in clothing that would show food hitting it," she said. "Each person had four of the same outfit so we could shoot numerous times. That's 120 costumes for one minute of film!"

- In Larry Tudgeman's fantasy, he imagines himself as Neo, the main character in the movie *The Matrix*.

- Downtown, Lanny eats vanilla ice cream, although in the first episode he ever appeared (#12 "Come Fly With Me"), he only ate pumpkin ice cream. (Nice to see he's learning to keep his options open!)

> Will someone confess already?!

CAN YOU SPOT THE BLOOPERS?

- In Lizzie's story, when Gustav is hit by food for the first time, he already has food all over his face.

- After the food fight, the amount of food on Lizzie's shirt varies from scene to scene.

EPISODE NUMBER 54:
"LIZZIE IN THE MIDDLE"

DIRECTOR: Savage Steve Holland
WRITERS: Nina G. Bargiel & Jeremy J. Bargiel
EXECUTIVE PRODUCERS: Stan Rogow & Susan Estelle Jansen
COEXECUTIVE PRODUCERS: Douglas Tuber & Tim Maile
SUPERVISING PRODUCER: Melissa Gould
PRODUCER: Jill Danton
SERIES CREATED BY: Terri Minsky
CAST STARS: Hilary Duff (Lizzie McGuire),
Lalaine (Miranda Sanchez),
Adam Lamberg
(David "Gordo" Gordon),
Jake Thomas (Matt McGuire),
Hallie Todd (Jo McGuire), and
Robert Carradine (Sam McGuire)
SPECIAL GUEST STAR: Frankie Muniz (Himself)
GUEST STARS: Clayton Snyder (Ethan Craft),
Kyle J. Downes (Larry Tudgeman),
Arvie Lowe, Jr. (Mr. Dig)
COSTARS: Bill La Mond (Reporter),
William Keane (Photographer)

WHAT HAPPENS?

In the middle of reading *Romeo & Juliet* with Ethan Craft, Lizzie is interrupted when *Malcolm in the Middle* star Frankie Muniz walks into her class. Frankie is instantly smitten with Lizzie and asks her out. She turns him down, knowing their two worlds are totally different. Later that night, Frankie comes by Lizzie's house and, after he plays board games with her parents, she agrees to go out with him. But it's not as fun as they'd hoped. On their first date, Lizzie must rescue Frankie from a mob of fans.

The next day, Lizzie is famous and everyone wants to know about her, so Matt makes the most of his sister's fame by giving tabloid reporters tours of her room.

Miranda and Gordo feel left out by Lizzie's new fame and new boyfriend. Even Lizzie can't handle the pressure anymore, and as she's about to break up with Frankie, he tells her he doesn't want to be responsible for ruining her life. Lizzie does get one last perk, though, when Frankie gives her a small role in his television movie.

DID YOU KNOW?

- Hilary Duff and Frankie Muniz are friends in real life and costarred in the 2003 movie *Agent Cody Banks*.

- Frankie's car, which he personally purchased after it appeared in the movie *The Fast & The Furious*, is shown in this episode.

- "Hey Juliet" by the band LMNT plays in this episode.

- On the movie marker shown in the scene when Frankie is shooting his TV movies, the director is listed as Savage Steve Holland and the cameraman is John Newby. They are the actual director and director of photography for this very episode of *Lizzie McGuire*.

Being famous is hard work.

CAN YOU SPOT THE BLOOPERS?

- When Frankie asks Lizzie out, a girl with a hot-pink backpack walks by, and in the next shot she walks by again.

- Lizzie gets a quadruple word score for "tween" when playing a board game. This isn't a recognized word in the dictionary.

EPISODE NUMBER 55:
"THE GREATEST CRUSH OF ALL"

DIRECTOR:	Rachel Feldman
WRITERS:	Douglas Tuber & Tim Maile
EXECUTIVE PRODUCERS:	Stan Rogow & Susan Estelle Jansen
COEXECUTIVE PRODUCERS:	Douglas Tuber & Tim Maile
SUPERVISING PRODUCER:	Melissa Gould
PRODUCER:	Jill Danton
SERIES CREATED BY:	Terri Minsky
CAST STARS:	Hilary Duff (Lizzie McGuire), Lalaine (Miranda Sanchez), Adam Lamberg (David "Gordo" Gordon), Jake Thomas (Matt McGuire), Hallie Todd (Jo McGuire), and Robert Carradine (Sam McGuire)
GUEST STARS:	Kyle J. Downes (Larry Tudgeman), Ashlie Brillault (Kate Sanders), Grant Thompson (Ewan Keith)
COSTARS:	Rachel Snow (Veruca), Jeremy Bargiel (Jeremy), David Alex Rosen (David), Lee Everett (Food Worker)

WHAT HAPPENS?

Lizzie and Miranda are totally in love with their new English teacher, Mr. Keith. Lizzie wants him to notice her, so she takes a special interest in his teaching, but she has stiff competition from Miranda. In fact, all of the girls in class love Mr. Keith, and they begin to fight over him.

Lizzie has big plans to watch Mr. Keith read poetry at a Scottish Festival, but she gets really upset when her parents make her take along Fredo the chimp. The McGuires are babysitting the chimp, and Lizzie is the only one Fredo likes.

Once Lizzie gets to the Festival, Fredo runs off just before Mr. Keith is about to read. Lizzie asks Miranda to help her rescue Fredo, who has climbed up a rope in the gym. The girls get to the gym just as Gordo has caught Fredo in his arms. When they get back to the festival, they find out a food fight has broken out over Mr. Keith, and because Lizzie and Miranda weren't involved he tells them he thinks they're mature. The girls think this is hilarious, considering how they fought over him—but they aren't about to tell him that!

DID YOU KNOW?

> Back off, girls. He's mine, all mine, totally mine!

- At the festival, Larry Tudgeman's face is painted purple because he is imitating the fierce Scottish warriors as they were portrayed in the Mel Gibson movie *Braveheart*.

- The original title of this episode was "My Love Is a Red, Red Chimp."

- In this episode, we learn that Gordo is part Scottish.

- Matt doesn't like Fredo because of the events in episode #36 "Mom's Best Friend," in which the chimp destroyed the McGuire house and Matt was blamed.

CAN YOU SPOT THE BLOOPERS?

- When Mr. Keith writes his name on the blackboard at the beginning of class, his name is underlined, but the line disappears and reappears from shot to shot.

- When Fredo is pulling at Gordo's ear, Gordo says "Ow," but as he walks out he still says "Ow," and Fredo's arms are clearly around his neck, not pulling his ear.

EPISODE NUMBER 56: "ONE OF THE GUYS"

DIRECTOR: Steve De Jarnatt
WRITERS: Nina G. Bargiel & Jeremy J. Bargiel
EXECUTIVE PRODUCERS: Stan Rogow & Susan Estelle Jansen
COEXECUTIVE PRODUCERS: Douglas Tuber & Tim Maile
SUPERVISING PRODUCER: Melissa Gould
PRODUCER: Jill Danton
SERIES CREATED BY: Terri Minsky
CAST STARS: Hilary Duff (Lizzie McGuire),
Lalaine (Miranda Sanchez),
Adam Lamberg
(David "Gordo" Gordon),
Jake Thomas (Matt McGuire),
Hallie Todd (Jo McGuire), and
Robert Carradine (Sam McGuire)
GUEST STARS: Ashlie Brillault (Kate Sanders),
Clayton Snyder (Ethan Craft),
Carly Schroeder (Melina Bianco),
Dot-Marie Jones (Coach Kelly),
Andrew McFarlane (Thomas)
COSTARS: Tonya Rowland (Ms. Chapman),
Phillip Blackwell (Quarterback),
Jeremy Bargiel (Jeremy),
David Alex Rosen (David)

WHAT HAPPENS?

In gym class, Lizzie sets the new school record for hanging from a bar. She beats Ethan, who is beginning to feel like less of a dude after being bested by a girl. At lunch, Ethan challenges Lizzie to an arm-wrestling contest and Lizzie wins again! Ethan and his friend Thomas think she's awesome, so they ask her to join their flag football game. She's excited about the idea of spending time with Ethan, so she says yes.

During the first game, Lizzie totally rocks and helps her team win. Ethan calls her a dude, and Thomas is equally impressed. That's when Kate makes fun of her for being boyish. Lizzie starts freaking out, thinking that the guys won't look at her as a girl, and she even has a nightmare about it. She decides to be more girly at school and quits the flag football team. Finally, she talks to Coach Kelly, who assures her that Kate is jealous and Ethan and Thomas think she's cool. Lizzie realizes Coach Kelly is right, so she joins the flag football game that day and her team wins!

DID YOU KNOW?

● This episode was ranked as the fifth-highest-rated of all the Lizzie telecasts. (Ratings were measured among kids ages 6 to 11 on November 21, 2003.)

I'm a total dude! (Not that there's anything wrong with that.)

● Lizzie says her girly outfit needs to be one part *Clueless* and two parts *Legally Blonde*, referring to the 1995 and 2001 fashion-conscious teen movies.

● The song "Supergirl" by Krystal plays when Lizzie is dressing up in her girly outfit for school.

CAN YOU SPOT THE BLOOPERS?

● Before Gordo falls off the bar, both of Lizzie's hands loosen on the bar, but she doesn't move.

● During her first game of flag football, Miranda and Gordo are on one end of the bleachers, and in the next shot, they are at the opposite end.

EPISODE NUMBER 57:
"GRAND OLE GRANDMA"

DIRECTOR:	Savage Steve Holland
WRITER:	Melissa Gould
EXECUTIVE PRODUCERS:	Stan Rogow & Susan Estelle Jansen
COEXECUTIVE PRODUCERS:	Douglas Tuber & Tim Maile
SUPERVISING PRODUCER:	Melissa Gould
PRODUCER:	Jill Danton
SERIES CREATED BY:	Terri Minsky
CAST STARS:	Hilary Duff (Lizzie McGuire), Lalaine (Miranda Sanchez), Adam Lamberg (David "Gordo" Gordon), Jake Thomas (Matt McGuire), Hallie Todd (Jo McGuire), and Robert Carradine (Sam McGuire)
SPECIAL GUEST STAR:	Doris Roberts (Grandma Ruth)

WHAT HAPPENS?

Gordo is excited about his grandmother coming to visit. He can't wait for her to make her famous brisket. But when he takes Lizzie and Miranda home to meet her, she's totally changed. She doesn't make brisket. Instead, she tries to get him to eat sushi and attempts to feng shui his living room. Gordo is confused. Who is this woman and what has she done with his grandmother?

Meanwhile, at the McGuire house, Lizzie's parents are sick in bed and Lizzie and Matt take advantage of the situation. They indulge on junk food and mess up the house.

At Gordo's place, after Grandma asks him to go snowboarding, he realizes how much he misses his old grandmother. Grandma goes to Lizzie's house to look for Gordo, and Lizzie tells her that sometimes kids just need a grandmother. Grandma Ruth realizes Lizzie is right, but first she puts the McGuire house back in order.

Back at Gordo's house, Grandma Ruth finally makes brisket. By this time, Mr. and Mrs. McGuire are feeling better, and when they come downstairs, they ground Lizzie and Matt for taking advantage of them!

DID YOU KNOW?

Strange but true: Grandmas can be way cool.

- Doris Roberts, who plays Grandma Ruth, stars on the CBS sitcom *Everybody Loves Raymond* as an overbearing mother.

- In this episode, Lizzie repeats the words we hear animated Lizzie say first. This is rarely done. Look for the scene where Grandma Ruth asks Lizzie if her parents are okay with Matt using all the sofa cushions. You'll hear animated Lizzie say, "They don't know!" And then Lizzie tells Grandma Ruth, "Actually, they don't know." Another time Lizzie repeats something that animated Lizzie says is during episode #13 "Random Acts of Miranda" when Lizzie exclaims, "Well, you're a lousy friend, too! And a stinkbag actress!"(after animated Lizzie says it first).

CAN YOU SPOT THE BLOOPERS?

- When Grandma Ruth is at school, an extra with an orange backpack walks by twice from the same direction in consecutive shots.

- In the opening scene, Gordo is sitting directly across from Miranda, and in the next shot, he's directly across from Lizzie.

119

EPISODE NUMBER 58:
"MY FAIR LARRY"

DIRECTOR:	Mark Rosman
WRITERS:	Nina G. Bargiel & Jeremy J. Bargiel
EXECUTIVE PRODUCERS:	Stan Rogow & Susan Estelle Jansen
COEXECUTIVE PRODUCERS:	Douglas Tuber & Tim Maile
SUPERVISING PRODUCER:	Melissa Gould
PRODUCER:	Jill Danton
SERIES CREATED BY:	Terri Minsky
CAST STARS:	Hilary Duff (Lizzie McGuire), Lalaine (Miranda Sanchez), Adam Lamberg (David "Gordo" Gordon), Jake Thomas (Matt McGuire), Hallie Todd (Jo McGuire), and Robert Carradine (Sam McGuire)
SPECIAL GUEST STARS:	Dabbs Greer (Moe), Eileen Brennan (Marge)
GUEST STARS:	Kyle J. Downes (Larry Tudgeman), Ashlie Brillault (Kate Sanders), Clayton Snyder (Ethan Craft), Carly Schroeder (Melina Bianco)
COSTARS:	Tonya Rowland (Ms. Chapman), Kathryn Kates (Mrs. Carrabino), Dan Swett (Security Guard)

WHAT HAPPENS?

Miranda is throwing a huge party, her first boy/girl bash, and she invites all the popular girls and guys at school—which does not include Larry Tudgeman. Lizzie thinks it's wrong that Larry is left out. But Miranda is stubborn and refuses to let Larry come, even though it becomes obvious that he wants to go.

Lizzie and Gordo decide to make over Larry into a cool mystery guy named "Lawrence" and sneak him into the party anyway. The disguise works so well that Larry actually looks like a hottie. Both Kate and Miranda are impressed with "Lawrence," and Miranda dances with him. When she's about to kiss him, Larry finally reveals his true identity, and Miranda screams! But, she finally realizes she was being a jerk and apologizes to Larry for not inviting him.

Meanwhile, Matt and Melina are assigned to a "Senior Pals" community service project by their teacher. They are paired up with two senior citizens from the retirement home. Neither couple is looking forward to their day together, but when they realize they are a lot alike, they have a prank-pulling blast.

DID YOU KNOW?

It's true love—doing a good deed!

- The title of this episode is based on the musical *My Fair Lady*, in which a poor girl is transformed into an aristocrat.

- When Miranda and Larry are dancing, the Britney Spears song "Not a Girl, Not Yet a Woman" plays.

- The year this episode first aired (2003), Lalaine, who plays Miranda, was honored as one of four finalists for the Imagen Award for Best Supporting Actress in Television. The other finalists were Constance Marie for *American Family*, Jacqueline Obradors for *NYPD Blue*, and Lana Parrilla for *Boomtown*, who won the award that year.

CAN YOU SPOT THE BLOOPERS?

- During the lunch scene, keep your eyes on a girl in a purple sweatshirt. She walks by Lizzie, Gordo, and Miranda in several different directions throughout several shots.

- Toward the end, a girl in a floral dress is dancing behind Larry and Miranda, and in the next shot, she's standing behind Gordo and Lizzie.

EPISODE NUMBER 59: "MY DINNER WITH DIG"

DIRECTOR:	Rusty Russ
WRITER:	Melissa Gould
EXECUTIVE PRODUCERS:	Stan Rogow & Susan Estelle Jansen
COEXECUTIVE PRODUCERS:	Douglas Tuber & Tim Maile
SUPERVISING PRODUCER:	Melissa Gould
PRODUCER:	Jill Danton
SERIES CREATED BY:	Terri Minsky
CAST STARS:	Hilary Duff (Lizzie McGuire), Lalaine (Miranda Sanchez), Adam Lamberg (David "Gordo" Gordon), Jake Thomas (Matt McGuire), Hallie Todd (Jo McGuire), and Robert Carradine (Sam McGuire)
GUEST STARS:	Arvie Lowe, Jr. (Mr. Dig), Carly Schroeder (Melina Bianco), Tonya Rowland (Ms. Chapman)

WHAT HAPPENS?

At lunch, Lizzie, Miranda, and Gordo discover that Mr. Dig eats only junk food. After giving him a lecture on proper nutrition, Miranda mentions that Lizzie's mom makes great meat loaf. Without thinking, Lizzie invites Mr. Dig to dinner at her house, and he accepts! The dinner goes well. In fact, Mr. McGuire and Mr. Dig become fast friends.

Later that week, Lizzie is really upset when she walks downstairs in an ugly facial mask and runs into Mr. Dig. It turns out that Mr. McGuire and Mr. Dig are good friends now, and they hang out all the time. Lizzie can't deal with seeing her teacher at home too, and asks her mom to talk to her dad. But after realizing that even her dad needs friends, she changes her mind.

Meanwhile, Matt's teacher Ms. Chapman is being tough on him. He thinks that if she and Mrs. McGuire become friends, maybe she'll be nicer. He invites Ms. Chapman to dinner, and it doesn't go well until Mr. Dig walks in. It turns out Ms. Chapman and Mr. Dig are old friends who've lost touch, so they both ditch the McGuire house for a private date.

DID YOU KNOW?

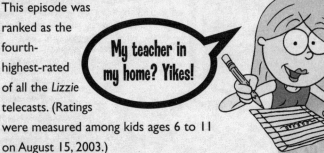

My teacher in my home? Yikes!

- This episode was ranked as the fourth-highest-rated of all the *Lizzie* telecasts. (Ratings were measured among kids ages 6 to 11 on August 15, 2003.)

- In this episode, both Gordo and Miranda say Mrs. McGuire is a great cook, but in previous episodes, she was known to be a bad cook. (Clearly, she took some cooking classes!)

- Mr. Dig's real name is Digby Sellers.

- Ms. Chapman's name is Jasmine Chapman.

CAN YOU SPOT THE BLOOPERS?

- When Mr. McGuire is talking to Gordo and Lizzie at school, the same extra in an orange shirt walks behind Lizzie in the same direction twice in a row.

- When Ms. Chapman tells the class to clear their desks, the girl behind Matt alternates between having nothing on her desk and having two books on her desk, from shot to shot.

- At dinner, Mr. McGuire obviously empties the bottle of dressing onto the salad, but in the next shot, the bottle is almost half full!

DIRECTOR: Robert Carradine
WRITERS: Douglas Tuber & Tim Maile
EXECUTIVE PRODUCERS: Stan Rogow & Susan Estelle Jansen
COEXECUTIVE PRODUCERS: Douglas Tuber & Tim Maile
SUPERVISING PRODUCER: Melissa Gould
PRODUCER: Jill Danton
SERIES CREATED BY: Terri Minsky
CAST STARS: Hilary Duff (Lizzie McGuire),
Lalaine (Miranda Sanchez),
Adam Lamberg
(David "Gordo" Gordon),
Jake Thomas (Matt McGuire),
Hallie Todd (Jo McGuire), and
Robert Carradine (Sam McGuire)
GUEST STARS: Kyle J. Downes (Larry Tudgeman),
Ashlie Brillault (Kate Sanders),
Clayton Snyder (Ethan Craft),
Carly Schroeder (Melina Bianco),
Joey Zimmerman (Soda Kid)
COSTARS: Kenneth Schmidt (Kid)

**EPISODE NUMBER 60:
"LIZZIE'S ELEVEN"**

WHAT HAPPENS?

As yearbook editor, Kate plans to fill the last spot in the yearbook with a picture of her and Ethan Craft at the school's "Monte Carlo" night. The *only* picture of Lizzie that Kate will put in the yearbook is an embarrassing shot of Lizzie with a rash. Lizzie thinks this is mean and unfair, so she, Gordo, Matt, and Melina hatch a scheme to foil Kate's plan.

As the DJ for "Monte Carlo" night, Lizzie pretends to get into a huge fight with Gordo. While Kate is distracted, Melina skillfully swaps Kate's purse for another just like it. Finally, Lizzie "messes up" and lets Kate know what's going on. Kate complains to Mrs. McGuire, and the two of them go to the back room to stop the kids' plan of switching the digital photo discs. Kate takes back her disc and delivers it to the printer right on time.

What Kate doesn't know is that Mrs. McGuire is in on Lizzie's plan, too, and she used her card dealer skills to switch the discs on Kate. Now, when the yearbook is handed out at school, everyone will see pictures of Lizzie instead of Kate!

DID YOU KNOW?

Kate, give it up. You don't stand a chance!

- Robert Carradine, who plays Mr. McGuire, directed this episode.

- Matt and Melina's schemes in this episode, especially their black outfits, were inspired by the Tom Cruise action film *Mission: Impossible*.

- The episode's title refers to the casino-caper movie *Ocean's Eleven*, a remake of the 1960s film *Ocean's 11*.

- Lizzie is allergic to oyster sauce. (Who knew?)

CAN YOU SPOT THE BLOOPERS?

- When Lizzie barges through the doors, they are blue, but from the interior, they are green.

- When Matt is giving Lizzie his list of demands for helping to trick Kate, Lizzie tosses her pink feather pen on the table before reading the paper. In one of the shots, though, she is holding both the paper and the pen in her hand.

EPISODE NUMBER 61:
"DEAR LIZZIE"

DIRECTOR: Mark Rosman
WRITERS: Nina G. Bargiel & Jeremy J. Bargiel
EXECUTIVE PRODUCERS: Stan Rogow & Susan Estelle Jansen
COEXECUTIVE PRODUCERS: Douglas Tuber & Tim Maile
SUPERVISING PRODUCER: Melissa Gould
PRODUCER: Jill Danton
SERIES CREATED BY: Terri Minsky
CAST STARS: Hilary Duff (Lizzie McGuire),
Lalaine (Miranda Sanchez),
Adam Lamberg
(David "Gordo" Gordon),
Jake Thomas (Matt McGuire),
Hallie Todd (Jo McGuire), and
Robert Carradine (Sam McGuire)
GUEST STARS: Clayton Snyder (Ethan Craft),
Ashlie Brillault (Kate Sanders),
Kyle J. Downes (Larry Tudgeman),
Carly Schroeder (Melina Bianco),
Simms Thomas (Ms. Dew),
Tonya Rowland (Ms. Chapman),
Davida Williams (Claire Miller),
Sean Marquette (Adam)

WHAT HAPPENS?

Lizzie wants to help Gordo with the school E-zine, so she becomes the Web site's advice columnist. The "Dear Lizzie" column is a huge hit. Lizzie is on a roll until some of her advice turns out badly. She-geek student Veruca asks Lizzie for advice on dealing with a bully. Lizzie tells Veruca to stand up to the bully, but it doesn't work. Lizzie realizes it's not easy giving advice. She decides to quit, but Gordo asks her to answer one last letter.

She's so rattled that she talks to her parents. Her dad tells her that she can't fix everything. Lizzie knows he's right, and she answers the letter. It's from "Confused Guy." He asks Lizzie what to do about his crush on his best friend. She tells him to tell her the truth. Lizzie never suspects that the letter is from Gordo and that he's talking about her! Gordo can't summon the courage to tell Lizzie how he feels, but he does tell her she gives good advice.

Meanwhile, at Matt's school, one of his fellow students is trying to take the glory for his pranks, but Matt won't stand for it. Along with Melina, he puts the wannabe in his place.

DID YOU KNOW?

- Simms Thomas, who plays flaky Ms. Dew, is the mother of Jake Thomas, who plays Matt.

Take my advice— don't try to give it!

- Kate Sanders has a body odor issue, which we discover when her fellow cheerleader Claire writes to Lizzie, asking for advice.

- When Lizzie imagines Larry taking over the world, he does so via an impression of the character Dr. Evil, seen in the Mike Myers movie *Austin Powers*.

- Miranda's absence in this episode is explained by Lizzie, who says she's sick.

CAN YOU SPOT THE BLOOPERS?

- Ethan signs his letter "More than good hair," but Lizzie writes back, "Dear Smarter."

- Gordo says Claire's letter is from "Queen Tween," but she signs off as "Clean Tween."

EPISODE NUMBER 62:
"THE GORDO SHUFFLE"

DIRECTOR: Steve De Jarnatt
WRITER: Melissa Gould
EXECUTIVE PRODUCERS: Stan Rogow & Susan Estelle Jansen
COEXECUTIVE PRODUCERS: Douglas Tuber & Tim Maile
SUPERVISING PRODUCER: Melissa Gould
PRODUCER: Jill Danton
SERIES CREATED BY: Terri Minsky
CAST STARS: Hilary Duff (Lizzie McGuire),
Lalaine (Miranda Sanchez),
Adam Lamberg
(David "Gordo" Gordon),
Jake Thomas (Matt McGuire),
Hallie Todd (Jo McGuire), and
Robert Carradine (Sam McGuire)
GUEST STAR: Kyle J. Downes (Larry Tudgeman),
Ashlie Brillault (Kate Sanders),
Clayton Snyder (Ethan Craft),
Carly Schroeder (Melina Bianco),
Davida Williams (Claire Miller)
COSTARS: Ricky Luna (Cashier),
Brian White (Pizza Guy),
Troy Rowland (Mr. Lang)

WHAT HAPPENS?

Gordo accidentally is mailed a credit card. He doesn't want to keep it, but Ethan convinces him to hold on to it. Gordo plans to only use it for emergencies, but he soon realizes he can use it to make a movie. Lizzie tries to talk him out of using the card, but he won't listen.

Gordo casts Ethan and Kate as the stars of his science-fiction movie, but nothing seems to go right. Gordo uses the card to charge everything from cameras to costumes, and he soon hits his limit when his card is declined by the pizza delivery guy. When his stars realize that there's no more money, they walk off the set. Gordo is left with no movie and a $5,000 credit card bill! He apologizes to Lizzie and tells her she was right.

Meanwhile, Matt's science fair is coming up, but he's not prepared. Even though he had weeks to put together a project, he waits until the last minute. In the end, Matt constructs a big elaborate project that makes . . . toast.

DID YOU KNOW?

🌼 Hilary Duff's dialogue coach, Troy Rowland, appears in this episode as Kate's dialogue coach.

Credit card + Gordo = big trouble!

🌼 When Matt and Melina are coming up with science fair ideas, the Oingo Boingo song "Weird Science" plays.

🌼 While filming Gordo's video, Larry Tudgeman is shown in a green shirt, not his usual putty-colored shirt with the green collar.

🌼 This episode's title is inspired by the 1987 Robert Townsend movie *The Hollywood Shuffle*.

🌼 Where is Miranda in this episode? She is on vacation.

CAN YOU SPOT THE BLOOPERS?

🌼 When Ethan, Gordo, and Lizzie are walking down the hall, a boy in a red-and-blue striped shirt passes by them going upstairs, and in the very next shot, he repeats the action.

🌼 When the pizza delivery guy holds Gordo's card, it's not signed on the back, even though it's been used multiple times.

DIRECTOR: Tim O'Donnell
WRITER: Bob Thomas
EXECUTIVE PRODUCERS: Stan Rogow & Susan Estelle Jansen
COEXECUTIVE PRODUCERS: Douglas Tuber & Tim Maile
SUPERVISING PRODUCER: Melissa Gould
PRODUCER: Jill Danton
SERIES CREATED BY: Terri Minsky
CAST STARS: Hilary Duff (Lizzie McGuire),
Lalaine (Miranda Sanchez),
Adam Lamberg
(David "Gordo" Gordon),
Jake Thomas (Matt McGuire),
Hallie Todd (Jo McGuire), and
Robert Carradine (Sam McGuire)
GUEST STARS: Clayton Snyder (Ethan Craft),
Ashlie Brillault (Kate Sanders),
Kyle J. Downes (Larry Tudgeman),
Rachel Snow (Veruca),
Haylie Duff (Cousin Amy),
Catherine Chiarelli (Ethan's Stepmom)

EPISODE NUMBER 63: "CLUE-LESS"

WHAT HAPPENS?

Ethan Craft is throwing a murder mystery party, but when his home is fumigated, Lizzie offers to have it at her house. Lizzie is excited to be cast as Penelope, the fiancée of Ethan's character. But Gordo stews because he says he'll be the guy no one notices—as usual. Lizzie tells him if he solves the mystery, he will get her attention. That's more than enough motivation for Gordo.

As the mystery begins, Lizzie is on a roll, but every time she finds a clue, Gordo tries to steal it. His competitive behavior starts to bug Lizzie until Kate breaks it down for her: Gordo is trying to win so Lizzie will notice him because he *likes* her. Lizzie freaks. She never suspected Gordo liked her! Just as Lizzie is about to reveal the identity of the killer, she purposely gives the wrong name so Gordo can win.

After everyone congratulates Gordo, Lizzie walks him to the door. Things are pretty weird between them now that Lizzie knows how he feels. Gordo is just about to ask Lizzie on a date when Mr. McGuire interrupts. The moment is gone, and Gordo goes home. Now Lizzie wonders what will happen between them.

DID YOU KNOW?

- Haylie Duff reappears in this episode as Kate's cousin Amy.

- Ethan Craft's stepmom is identified as "Tawny," and like Ethan, she's depicted as a clueless hottie.

- Miranda is still "out of town" in this episode.

- The characters that the cast members play at the murder mystery party are the following: Lizzie (Penelope Featherstone); Ethan (Clyde McGuffin); Gordo (Aubrey Carstairs); Jo McGuire (The Maid); Sam McGuire (Lord McGuffin); Kate (Esme Upshaw); Amy (Desiree Fireberry); Larry (Guy Gaviotta); Veruca (Fiona St. John).

Bring it on, Nancy Drew!

CAN YOU SPOT THE BLOOPERS?

- At school, a boy in a Hawaiian shirt walks down the stairs behind Ethan, and in the next shot he's walking toward the stairs in the opposite direction.

- When Gordo pulls the paper that says "Penelope" from the hat, it's in his right hand, but as he's about to pull another name out of the hat, the first paper disappears.

EPISODE NUMBER 64:
"XTREME XMAS"

DIRECTOR:	Savage Steve Holland
WRITERS:	Douglas Tuber & Tim Maile
EXECUTIVE PRODUCERS:	Stan Rogow & Susan Estelle Jansen
COEXECUTIVE PRODUCERS:	Douglas Tuber & Tim Maile
SUPERVISING PRODUCER:	Melissa Gould
PRODUCER:	Jill Danton
SERIES CREATED BY:	Terri Minsky
CAST STARS:	Hilary Duff (Lizzie McGuire), Lalaine (Miranda Sanchez), Adam Lamberg (David "Gordo" Gordon), Jake Thomas (Matt McGuire), Hallie Todd (Jo McGuire), and Robert Carradine (Sam McGuire)
SPECIAL GUEST STAR:	Steven Tyler (Santa Claus)
GUEST STARS:	Shelley Berman (Nobby), Kyle J. Downes (Larry Tudgeman), Ashlie Brillault (Kate Sanders), Haylie Duff (Cousin Amy)
COSTARS:	David Alex Rosen (David), Jeremy Bargiel (Jeremy), Samantha Smith (Nine-year-old), Austin W. Glenn (Thirteen-year-old), Brad Grunberg (Announcer), Troy Rowland (Mr. Lang), Jackson Rogow (Kid), Chelsea Tallirico (Bystander #1), Taj Tallirico (Bystander #2)

WHAT HAPPENS?

Lizzie is determined to win this year's Christmas parade float contest. With her family and Gordo's help, she sets out to build a "Rock 'n' Roll Christmas" float. But her parents take time out to have dinner with Nobby—a nutty old man who thinks he's one of Santa's elves.

When the plumbing breaks at Nobby's retirement home, Mr. and Mrs. McGuire, Matt, and Gordo all pitch in to help fix it. Lizzie is furious. Everyone has abandoned her float! A tired Lizzie dozes off and has a dream where everyone asks her why she's forgotten the true meaning of Christmas—helping others.

When Lizzie wakes, she realizes she was wrong. She rushes to help her family, saving the day and Nobby's plumbing. On Christmas morning, she's shocked to see her finished float coming down the street in the parade! It's beautiful, and riding on it, singing his heart out, is Steven Tyler of Aerosmith! Everyone is wowed, but Lizzie is stumped. Who finished her float? Nobby introduces her to a guy with a white beard and a red suit. Looks like Nobby travels in some pretty cool circles after all!

Christmas spirit? I'm all over it.

DID YOU KNOW?

- Steven Tyler of the rock band Aerosmith plays the singing Santa in this episode.

- Hilary met Steven Tyler and his daughter at a movie premiere. Because Tyler's daughter was a big fan of the *Lizzie McGuire* television series, their connection led to the idea that Tyler might make a special appearance on the show.

- Tyler's children, Chelsea Tallirico and Taj Tallirico, also appear in this episode.

- Executive Producer Stan Rogow says that next to the series pilot (episode #1 Pool Party) this was one of the most challenging episodes to film because of the big production of the parade and the musical performance on camera.

- Haylie Duff, Hilary's sister, appears once again as Cousin Amy.

- Mr. McGuire's cousin ReeRee can be seen in the Christmas parade.

CAN YOU SPOT THE BLOOPERS?

- When Nobby introduces himself to the McGuires, Mr. McGuire calls him "Notty."

- When Steven Tyler performs at the end of the episode, his microphone changes positions from being on its stand to off its stand from shot to shot.

133

DIRECTOR: Ken Ceizler

WRITER: Jaime Becker

EXECUTIVE PRODUCERS: Stan Rogow & Susan Estelle Jansen

COEXECUTIVE PRODUCERS: Douglas Tuber & Tim Maile

SUPERVISING PRODUCER: Melissa Gould

PRODUCER: Jill Danton

SERIES CREATED BY: Terri Minsky

CAST STARS: Hilary Duff (Lizzie McGuire),
Lalaine (Miranda Sanchez),
Adam Lamberg
(David "Gordo" Gordon),
Jake Thomas (Matt McGuire),
Hallie Todd (Jo McGuire), and
Robert Carradine (Sam McGuire)

GUEST STARS: Clayton Snyder (Ethan Craft),
Kyle J. Downes (Larry Tudgeman),
Ashlie Brillault (Kate Sanders),
Carly Schroeder (Melina Bianco),
Phill Lewis (Principal Tweedy)

COSTARS: Troy Rowland (Mr. Lang),
Mitchah Williams (Student #1),
Sarah Kapp (Student #2),
Rory Shoaf (Photographer)

EPISODE NUMBER 65: "BYE, BYE HILLRIDGE JUNIOR HIGH"

WHAT HAPPENS?

It's the last day of junior high and Lizzie can't wait to go to high school in the fall. But when she gets to school, she finds a flyer from the high school seniors on her locker designed to scare the junior high graduates. Then Kate says something typically mean to Lizzie, and Lizzie starts to feel like a loser. Gordo assures her that she's great.

When the class gets their yearbooks, Lizzie and Gordo go over the pictures, remembering how much fun they had in junior high. Gordo also regrets never telling Lizzie that he likes her. He recalls their moments together while trying to figure out the perfect thing to write in her yearbook. Finally, he writes: "Dear Lizzie, You rock. Don't ever change. And only I really mean it." When Lizzie reads it, she realizes that Gordo has been a great friend, and with him at her side, high school will be a blast. Just as Principal Tweedy is about to snap the class picture, Lizzie leans over and kisses Gordo on the cheek. Aww!

DID YOU KNOW?

High school, here I come!

- At the end of the episode, the song "I Can't Wait" plays. It's performed by Hilary Duff.

- Miranda has taken an early vacation to Mexico in this episode, which explains her absence.

- Ethan plans on playing water polo in high school.

- Executive Producer Stan Rogow says that next to the series pilot (episode #1 Pool Party) and episode #64 "X-treme X-mas," this was the most difficult of episodes to work on, simply because it was so sad for everyone to be filming the very last episode.

CAN YOU SPOT THE BLOOPERS?

- Right after Mr. McGuire goes to Lizzie's bedroom and asks "Can I come in," Lizzie is lying at the foot of the bed, and in the next quick shot, she's sitting at the head of the bed, then in the next shot, she's at the foot of the bed again.

- In the yearbook, "embarrassing" is spelled incorrectly (with one "s" instead of two)!

- Lizzie is at school, but Matt is at home, making a pool in the basement. Why isn't he in school? Hmmm . . .

135

THE LIZZIE MCGUIRE MOVIE

WALT DISNEY PICTURES
A STAN ROGOW PRODUCTION
RELEASE DATE: MAY 2. 2003

DIRECTOR: Jim Fall
WRITERS: Susan Estelle Jansen & Ed Decter & John J. St
PRODUCER: Stan Rogow
COPRODUCER: Susan Estelle Jansen
EXECUTIVE PRODUCERS: David Roessell & Terri Minsky
CAST: Hilary Duff (Lizzie McGuire/Isabella Parigi),
Adam Lamberg (David "Gordo" Gordon),
Robert Carradine (Sam McGuire),
Hallie Todd (Jo McGuire),
Jake Thomas (Matt McGuire),
Yani Gellman (Paolo Valisari),
Alex Borstein (Miss Ungermeyer),
Clayton Snyder (Ethan Craft),
Ashlie Brillault (Kate Sanders),
Brendan Kelly (Sergei),
Carly Schroeder (Melina Bianco),
Daniel R. Escobar (Mr. Escobar),
Jody Racicot (Giorgio),
Terra MacLeod (Franca DiMontecatini),
Claude Knowlton (Stage Manager),
Katy Saunders (Cute Girl #1),
Antonio Cupo (Model #2)

WHAT HAPPENS?

After graduating junior high, Lizzie flies off on a class trip to
Rome! While touring around the city, Lizzie is approached by a
gorgeous Italian guy, who tells her she looks just like a famous
Italian pop singer named Isabella. The Italian guy turns out to be
Isabella's singing partner, Paolo, who says he and Isabella have
broken up. Gordo wants Lizzie to be happy, so he convinces her
to say yes when Paolo asks her out. Lizzie lies to the school
chaperone, pretending to be sick so she can sneak off to tour the
city with Paolo.

Then Paolo convinces Lizzie to pretend to be Isabella at a
major music event that will be televised worldwide. Lizzie agrees,
but just when her scheme is about to be discovered, Gordo
sacrifices himself, telling the chaperone that Lizzie has been cov-
ering for him. Gordo is kicked off the trip. But, just as he's about
to board the plane home, he sees the real Isabella at the airport

Good-bye, home; hello, Rome!

- At the beginning of the movie, Lizzie is lip-synching to "The Tide Is High," sung by British girl group Atomic Kitten (and originally recorded by Blondie).

- Characters missing from the movie who were regularly seen in the TV series: Miranda, Claire, Larry, and Lanny.

- Miranda does not go to Rome, because she is in Mexico City on vacation.

and discovers the truth about Paolo. Gordo and Isabella race to the music event and stop Paolo from making a fool of Lizzie on stage. Paolo's plan was to show the world that Isabella couldn't sing, but the truth is that Paolo is the bad singer. Backstage, Isabella sings for Lizzie—and she wows everyone.

Later at the hotel, Lizzie takes Gordo up to the roof to talk. First, he took the fall for her, and then he saved her from embarrassing herself in front of the whole world. Is there any better friend in the universe? No, Lizzie decides, and kisses him! Now she's not just starting high school with her best friend— she's starting it with the best boyfriend a girl could ever have.

CAST BIOGRAPHIES

HILARY DUFF
"Lizzie McGuire"

Born September 28, 1987, Hilary Duff is a native of Houston, Texas. She made her stage debut at age six when she landed a spot in *The Nutcracker* as part of the BalletMet Columbus touring company. Her subsequent role in a television commercial spurred her longing to act and she soon amassed several television and film credits.

A dynamic young star, Hilary played the title role in all sixty-five episodes of Disney Channel's international hit series *Lizzie McGuire* as well as the lead role in Disney Channel's original movie *Cadet Kelly*, which ranked as cable television's highest rated movie in 2002.

In August 2002, the talented Duff crossed over to other platforms, making her singing debut with the single "I Can't Wait" on the *Lizzie McGuire* sound track, which was inspired by the hit TV series. The song quickly catapulted up the charts on Radio Disney and the sound track went certified platinum. Hilary's successful singing debut was then followed by her own Christmas-themed album, *Santa Claus Lane*, released by Walt Disney Records.

In 2003, Hilary starred in Disney's feature film *The Lizzie McGuire Movie*, which also spun off a certified platinum sound track that included songs sung by Hilary. That year, she also appeared in the movies *Agent Cody Banks*, costarring Frankie Muniz, and *Cheaper by the*

Dozen, starring Steve Martin and Bonnie Hunt. In the fall of 2003, Hilary launched another album, *Metamorphosis*.

"I like to work," Hilary told *TV Guide* in a 2003 interview. "[My life] is very crazy and busy," she also acknowledged in an MTV interview, "but I love it that way. And I love to be on the edge and have so much stuff to do."

In 2004, Hilary starred in the movie *A Cinderella Story*, began filming the movies *Heart of Summer* and *A Perfect Man*, and launched a summer music tour. Stay tuned—there's sure to be more on the big screen and on the music charts from Hilary!

Hilary's honors include a Young Artist Award for Best Supporting Actress for her appearance in the 1999 television movie *Soul Collector*. She was also honored with a nomination as Favorite Television Actress for Nickelodeon's 16th Annual Kids' Choice Awards and accepted the award for the *Lizzie McGuire* show, which was voted Favorite Television Series at the event—as it had been the year before.

You can see Hilary in the movies *Playing by Heart* with Sean Connery, and in the Cannes Film Festival favorite *Human Nature* with Tim Robbins. In the successful video release *Casper Meets Wendy*, check out Hilary as the friendly ghost's best friend, Wendy.

Hilary splits her time between homes in Houston and Los Angeles with her parents, her actress/singer/songwriter sister, Haylie, who has appeared in several episodes of *Lizzie McGuire*, and her two dogs. Hilary enjoys swimming, tumbling, and Rollerblading. She has also served on the Advisory Board of the Audrey Hepburn Child Benefit Fund and the Celebrity Council of Kids with a Cause.

LALAINE
"Miranda Sanchez"

Born June 3, 1987, in Burbank, California, Lalaine started her stage career at the age of ten when she was cast in the national touring company of *Les Miserables*. Roles in television movies followed, including *Annie*, which won the Emmy Award for best television movie and was produced for ABC's *The Wonderful World of Disney*. Lalaine's other television movies include *Borderline* and *Mrs. Santa Claus*.

Lalaine's role in the *Lizzie McGuire* TV series led her to star in the Disney Channel original movie *You Wish!*, which led to a hit recording of the title song. In 2003, Lalaine was honored as one of four finalists for the Imagen Award for Best Supporting Actress in Television.

Lalaine's feature film credits include the Robert Duvall film *The Apostle*, director Adrian Lyne's *Lolita*, and *Babe: Pig in the City*, in which she had a voice role.

Lalaine enjoys dancing, figure skating, horseback riding, basketball, swimming, and, of course, singing. She has already launched a recording career and is at work on her first album. She currently resides in Los Angeles.

ADAM LAMBERG
"Gordo"

Born in New York City on
September 14, 1984, Adam
Lamberg grew up as a regular
kid going to public school. When he was
seven, he auditioned and won the part in an
American Express commercial. After that, he
says he became hooked on acting. He soon appeared in the
feature film *I'm Not Rappaport* (1996) and the TV movie *Radiant
City* with Kirstie Alley (1996).

Then came the role of Gordo in Disney Channel's *Lizzie
McGuire* series. "I like to think I am a 'down to earth kind of guy'
like Gordo," Adam has been quoted as saying, but he adds,
"although Gordo is kind of dorky at times."

Adam has appeared in such telefilms and miniseries as TNT's
The Day Lincoln Was Shot, in which he portrayed Tad Lincoln and
Larry McMurtry's *Dead Man's Walk*. He also has appeared on the
daytime dramas *Another World* and *Guiding Light*.

In addition to starring in *The Lizzie McGuire Movie*, in which he
reprised his role as Gordo, Adam can be seen in the film *When
Do We Eat?* On stage, Adam has starred in many productions,
including *Macbeth*, *The Gathering*, *Asylum*, and Eric Bogosian's
Griller. Adam enjoys playing tennis and basketball. He is currently
attending college in Berkeley, California.

ROBERT CARRADINE
"Sam McGuire"

Robert Carradine, a native of
Hollywood, California, is part of a
legendary acting family that
includes his father, John
Carradine, and half-brothers David and
Keith Carradine. Robert made his big-screen
debut in the famous John Wayne movie *The
Cowboys* and has appeared in many film and television
productions throughout his career. Of his many roles, Robert's
best known was as head nerd Lewis Skolnik in the 1984 feature
film comedy *Revenge of the Nerds*. While acting in *Lizzie McGuire*,
Robert directed an episode (#60 "Lizzie's Eleven"). For Disney
Channel, he also appeared in the original movie *Mom's Got a Date
with a Vampire*. And, of course, he plays Lizzie's dad in *The Lizzie
McGuire Movie*.

HALLIE TODD
"Jo McGuire"

California native Hallie Todd first
rose to fame in the Amy
Heckerling-directed
blockbuster teen comedy *Fast Times at*

Ridgemont High. Before joining the cast of *Lizzie McGuire*, she also starred in the television shows *Life With Roger* and *Going Places.* Hallie appeared in the Disney Channel original movie *The Ultimate Christmas Present*, and she reprised her role as Jo McGuire in *The Lizzie McGuire Movie.* As a guest star, she has appeared in such series as *Murder One*, *Brooklyn Bridge*, and *Star Trek: The Next Generation.*

JAKE THOMAS
"Matt McGuire"

Jake was born January 30, 1990, in Knoxville Tennessee. When he was six, his family moved to Hollywood, California, where he became an accomplished young actor. Jake has appeared in the feature film *A.I.: Artificial Intelligence* with Haley Joel Osment and in *The Cell* with Jennifer Lopez. He has also made guest appearances on the television series *3rd Rock From the Sun* and *Touched by an Angel.* He lives in southern California with his parents, who are also in the entertainment business. (His father, Bob Thomas, wrote Lizzie episodes #48 "Best Dressed for Much Less" and #51 "Bunkies.") When not in school or working, Jake enjoys swimming, riding his scooter on and off the set, and collecting trading cards.

Stan Rogow—Executive Producer

Brooklyn, New York, native Stan Rogow attended law school before going into television. Stan also cocreated and produced the series *Shannon's Deal*, *Middle Ages*, *South of Sunset*, the ABC Family series *State of Grace*, and *The Lizzie McGuire Movie*. Of developing *Lizzie McGuire*, he says, "This series is really all about that moment in time when kids are wondering what, and how, and who to become. We're taking one of the most formative periods in a person's life and comically examining the experiences—good and bad, easy and difficult."

Susan Estelle Jansen—Executive Producer

Susan Jansen is an experienced television writer and producer. In addition to *Lizzie McGuire*, Susan produced and wrote *Boy Meets World* and wrote episodes of *Home Improvement*. Susan also produced *The Lizzie McGuire Movie*.

Terri Minsky—Creator

Along with creating *Lizzie McGuire*, Terri Minsky created *The Geena Davis Show* on ABC. Terri also produced series such as *Flying Blind* for FOX, and she was a consultant on HBO's *Sex and the City*. Terri also produced *The Lizzie McGuire Movie*.